Determining Factor
Conformation = Universal Peace

Elaine Reeves

DEDICATION

I want to dedicate this book to my wonderful husband who supported me through every step of the process. His godly influence has kept me focused on the gift that God has given me, and the message that He has given me to share. I also want to thank my sister Lisa, my number one fan, for helping and encouraging me to complete this work.

CONTENTS

PROLOGUE

2091…. How long man has walked the earth and still has retained his barbaric nature. The lawgivers declare this to be an age of great technological advancement and social order…just a pretty cover for an invidious truth.

Loneliness, hopelessness, despair…well, they all still walk the streets. The only thing different since the new Order has been in place is the packaging. They're all locked up tight in a prison of fear imposed by the Committee…where one slip up..one infraction of the law brings judgment…and with judgment…death.

1
JUDGMENT DAY

Justin Walker stood at the top of the steps overlooking Courthouse Plaza; steel and cement as far as the eye could see. The centerpiece of all this construction towered behind him; it was the city's courthouse. Its mirrored surface reflected the deserted plaza below. Periodically someone would exit a building and scurry along to the next or pull up in a secure vehicle and be escorted inside. It was so dreary and depressing; Justin wondered how any human being could stand working in the place. The dismal atmosphere seemed to suck the life out of everything, even the hot August sun. It's warmth was snatched right out of the air.

Besides the massive courthouse building, there stood the Pennsylvania Educational Center, office buildings for city security and the corrector's living quarters. If you didn't work here, weren't sent to the educational facilities for reprogramming, or were called before the judge, it's safe to say you would never set foot in the place. Most people didn't know what the plaza looked like unless they were in trouble; by then it was really too late to even care. It plaza was located at the center of town and was duplicated in every major city in the world.

Justin only had a few minutes to collect his

thoughts before he would be ushered inside. He leaned heavily on his left leg trying to alleviate the throbbing pain in the right one. Although the doctors released him into the custody of the correctors, he was far from being healed. In fact, just hours ago he was lying in a hospital bed with tubes stuck in his arm. He still couldn't figure out why they would save his life only to take it later. But there was no arguing with how this government did business. If you did, you'd be standing right where Justin was.

Taking slow, deep breaths, Justin tried to manage the pain and mentally prepare himself for the hearing. Being called before the "Committee" was something every man, woman, and child feared....a fear which had been instilled within them since birth. Today was judgment day for Justin Walker and he knew no one had ever made it through with their life.

It hadn't always been like this...the "Committee" wasn't always in existence. Law abiding men and woman once had the freedom to live their lives and make their own choices. They didn't have to look over their shoulders fearing retaliation from their own government. A piece of literary genius, "The Constitution of the United States", was written in 1787 and became part of the American way of life in 1789. Now, over three hundred years later, no one had ever seen the parchment and its carefully inscribed promises. The document once kept safe and protected was burned along with many other books and documents the new order considered inappropriate for the new age. No need to fill the heads of their citizens with foolish things like hope, independence, and freedom. There was a better way to live now and the government was there to make sure you didn't step outside the boundaries they set.

From what his parents told him, before they were judged, the big change started shortly before the year 2000. Prior to this, computers began showing up in more and more homes; the world soon developed a strong reliance on technology. Scientists everywhere were convinced the system was on the brink of collapse due to the imbedded calendar. We would lose power, heat, water, all the necessities. In addition, machines everywhere would crash causing airplanes to fall out of the sky or never be able to take off at all. Trains, cars, anything and everything with any type of chip or circuit board were destined to fail….even your electric toothbrush. During that time many people were convinced that the end was coming and preachers everywhere were announcing doom. After all, they professed, this generation was full of sin and society had degraded so rapidly….well there was no hope for this lost generation.

Of course, the lawmakers of the time jumped at

the opportunity. There had been rumors of the United Nation's desire for a one-world government for years. Most shrugged off the rumors as paranoid delusions of the far right political party. Other's blamed a crazy religious sect called Christians for the baseless rumors. There was always a reason and someone to blame so most people ignored all the signs. And just like other events throughout history, by the time people became aware it was already too late.

The truth of the matter was the United States had been in a spiraling decline for about a decade prior to all of this. The country as a whole had become sick of the ongoing problems in government; financial crisis, embassy bombings, and media bias had become the norm. Making matters worse was the country's standing in the foreign arena. As America descended further into the hole of immorality and greed, the rest of the world watched. Soon we no longer held their respect and became the target of terrorist groups that were positioned around the world; some even in our own back yards. The once great country teetered at the brink of collapse and the government officials were too busy fighting amongst themselves to actually figure out a solution to the problem. At first people seemed to be oblivious to what was going on but, as time went on, their eyes began to open to the corruption taking place. They began speaking out and orchestrating public demonstrations; as time passed and nothing was gained, the protests became more violent. In attempt to squelch the outcry of national dissatisfaction, the government tried to seize more and more control sending the country to the brink of another civil war.

The United States wasn't the only country having its difficulties. The Middle East had erupted with terrorist activity and thousands were being killed every month. In addition to the violence, twenty-five European countries had collapsed financially causing the global market to take a dive.

Adam Greiss was a young presidential candidate out of Alabama. He was a true family man; married for thirty years with three children and a dog. He appeared to be sympathetic to the plight of the American people and sincere in his desire for change. The American people ate up every word he said like a savory dessert. In their eyes he was going to save them all. Election time came and he won with a landslide.

The new president of the United States, Adam Greiss, had only just been elected two months prior to the chaos. Justin's grandfather told him the country had put all their hope in this one man. Despite their dissatisfaction with the government in general, the people believed that Greiss stood for something different; something wholesome and good. Americans were desperate for change and that was what he promised to bring them.

January 1, 2000, President Greiss woke up to business as usual. He got his morning cup of coffee and went to the oval office and sat in the leather chair at his desk. Spinning it to face the window he sipped on his warm brew waiting for his phone to ring. For a world in chaos President Greiss found the morning extremely peaceful. A call did eventually come but it wasn't what he expected; a meeting with the United Nations and a new job description.

It was the first time in the history of mankind that global unity took place. Behind the scenes during the last few months leading up to the new millennium, the United Nations began producing new laws to replace the old. A new order was created and America, along with the rest of the world, was led blindly right into it.

The acting presidents, prime ministers, kings and queens of every foreign land retained their titles and positions. But, of course, they were only token figures and had no real power. In reality all governing power was bestowed upon the new head of the United Nations, Gustov Baccus. If you ask anyone who Gustov Baccus really is, it's next to impossible to get a straight answer. No one knows for sure. He just quietly rose up through the ranks while everyone's attention was on the world's problems. When he finally had the ear of the elite and powerful, he began to spin a web of lies that appealed to their greed and lust for power. One by one they began to seek him out for every little decision until the whole of the United Nations sought out his word and guidance. There wasn't anyone in the United Nations who challenged him when he finally took over power. They were mesmerized at the thoughts of their dream being realized. Once in control, Baccus formed the "Committee" followed by the enforcers known as the "Correctors of Society" or "Correctors" for short.

The Correctors always traveled in pairs and were everywhere...protecting the unity of the new world and correcting anyone who failed to obey the law.

Gone were the days when you would drive down the highway and be barraged with fast food signs or store advertisements. Now, it was all government all the time. You couldn't leave your house, turn on the television or any other electronic device without seeing the universal slogan, "Conformation=Universal Peace" or some other government message. It was plastered everywhere to remind the public...one mistake and you're out. Out of what they considered to be a perfect society. Yes, it is true no one knows what goes on behind closed doors but no one could escape the eyes of the correctors for very long. Some went out of their way to watch and report any infraction in the hopes they would be looked upon as a valued citizen. Eventually they all outlived their usefulness.

Ironically, if left alone, everything would have transitioned into the new millennium without a glitch. There were no computer crashes, no interruptions in utilities or public transportation. It was the same as it always was...or it would have been. Unfortunately, mankind had a habit of making problems out of nothing and then sitting complacent until the government bailed them out. And the governments; well they were more than eager to take on the job.

"I guess I should consider myself lucky," Justin's mind reasoned. He had gotten further and lived through more than most men the age of thirty-three. In fact, Justin believed he was a walking miracle. Somehow that still didn't comfort him. He shook his head thinking, "No, I don't think any day would be a good day to die, especially like this."

This train of thought was abruptly ended when two correctors came up behind him, each grabbing an elbow. These were the same two thugs that gave him the ride to the courthouse from the hospital. They were there to make sure Justin didn't escape justice; or what they called justice.

They roughly pushed him towards the entrance of the courthouse and through the secured electronic double doors.

"Watch it!" Justin said in a combination of anger and pain," If you don't, you'll be carrying me in."

Neither one bothered to respond but they did relax their hold a little and slowed their pace. I'm sure the last thing they wanted to do was injure him and have to take him back to the hospital. They had postponed the hearing long enough.

Once inside, they let him go so they could take care of verifying his documents with the registrant. Welcoming the reprieve, Justin slumped down into a nearby chair. He felt horrible; all the energy seemed to have drained from his body. The throbbing in his head was keeping beat with the one in his leg. Justin closed his eyes and leaned his head back against the wall. Unfortunately the rest was short lived. "Come on Walker, we don't have all day."

Justin opened his eyes and slowly got to his feet. The room began spinning almost immediately causing him to reach out and touch the wall in an attempt to steady himself. He squeezed his eyes closed for a few more seconds and, when he opened them again, the spinning stopped and he was able to continue on. The correctors had backed off a little since they entered the building; he wasn't going to go anywhere now. They just walked behind him keeping pace.

The inside of the courthouse was quiet...almost eerily so. No one was allowed to enter without the committee's permission and they usually restricted access to those being judged, witnesses and of course the correctors. On the way to the Courtroom of Conviction they passed two androids patrolling the area, but that was all Justin saw. They were careful to keep all witnesses away from the accused...it was a shock tactic. You never knew what or who to expect...it was just another mind game the committee played with its prey.

As they approached the courtroom, two massive oak doors swung open by some unseen force. Justin limped forward across the threshold and immediately came face to face with the "Committee".

"Oh...man." Justin sighed. It was like something out of a bad horror flick. Six men and one elderly women sat stone faced behind a long black marble desk. Five of them were dressed in the black robes of their office. The sixth committee member, small but dignified in appearance, wore a gray robe with red trim. He was the supreme judge and in control of the entire process. Off to the right sat a mousy looking man of about twenty-five. Greasy dark hair fell across his forehead and his small black eyes darted back and forth nervously. From the look of the equipment surrounding him, Justin figured he must be the person in charge of recording the proceedings and recalling facts from the Global Life History Bank. Although not impressive to look at, he was considered an important man. Those who served in this manner had little if any contact with the outside world. This guaranteed the information they had access to would remain safe and uncorrupted. In addition, it guaranteed that they would have their man around for many years...it was unheard of for anyone who served as part of the "Committee" or part of its workings to ever be judged. However, it had been known to happen from time to time when a committee member lost his or her sanity and had to be committed to the state ward, never to be seen again. All that time being cut off from the world, deciding the fate of every person who walked through the doors; the stress was enough to push even the strongest of character over the proverbial edge.

Justin glanced around at his surroundings as he was ushered to the center of the room and made to sit in an uncomfortable metal chair. The air conditioning was blasting and the temperature of the room was an uncomfortable sixty degrees. This added to the aching in Justin's leg. He rubbed his knee lightly using the friction to warm it. The circular room was without windows and its light came from a large solar disc in the ceiling. That combined with the pale color of the room made an awful glare causing him to squint in order to see his accusers. Empty replicas of the chair he sat in lined the wall's perimeter.

"Mr. Walker, will you stand up and face the committee," the supreme judge ordered.

Justin came to his feet slowly, his leg stiff and sore.

"According to the laws established in the Global Unity Act of 2000, I am obligated to read you the following," he said and then took a sip of water from the glass on the table in front of him. Placing it back down, he slowly read the passage. "We hereby accuse you Justin Walker of refusing to conform to the laws and thereby becoming a danger to society. You will be judged in this courtroom today and if found guilty, led to the Cleansing Room where you will be put to death. Do you understand what you've been told?"

"Yes," Justin replied faintly before limping back to his seat and plopping down awkwardly. There was no need for any formal introduction into the hearing...it began immediately with the first witness. Justin groaned inwardly as he saw Thomas Mannan step from behind a hidden partition on the other side of the desk. Mannan was Justin's boss up until a few months ago. Justin knew he would be testifying but nothing could prepare him for how difficult it would be to look him in the face. Mannan seemed just as uncomfortable; he adjusted his tie repeatedly and refused to even look in Justin's direction.

Mannan walked over to stand in front of the committee to be sworn in. The speaker, the only woman sitting on the committee, stood up and began to recite the terms of the pledge he was expected to agree to. "Do you Thomas Mannan swear to tell the truth, the whole truth, and nothing but the truth. Do you swear by the Global Unity Act of 2000 to reveal any action taken by the accused that does not conform to this law?"

"I do," he replied and then cleared his throat nervously.

"Go stand next to Mr. Phillips," she gestured towards the man behind all the machinery. "He'll show you what to do next."

"Don't be nervous sir," Mr. Phillips reassured him as he positioned Mannan near the wall. Sitting back down he gave a numeric command to the computer...Mannan was instantly surrounded by a dim blue light. "This will enable accurate readings to be picked up by the computer for recording purposes," he explained, "It also reads eye movement, breathing patterns, and pulse rate to ensure the testimony given is true and to the best of your knowledge. Just relax," he added seeing the anxiety in his eyes.

"OK, enough of this!" the supreme judge

bellowed, "We have ten more cases to hear...let's get on with it!"

"Ok, ok," Mannan stammered nervously, "Justin worked for me until recently."

"Go on," the speaker encourage impatiently.

"He tried to steal top secret government technology from my company." Mannan seemed reluctant to divulge any information.

"What exactly did he steal?" another committee member questioned.

"Well I can't say because it's top secret." He continued uncomfortably.

"You need to be more specific, nothing will leave this courtroom," urged the speaker.

"It was a chip, something he was working on," Mannan answered, unconsciously running a finger along his shirt collar as if trying to loosen it.

"You say it was a government contract?" the committee member at the far end of the table piped in. He was extremely thin; his features elongated and almost coming to a sharp point. Justin thought he reminded him of a bird the way that he moved in small clipped motions as he jotted down notes.

"Ahh yes, yes sir I did," Mannan replied.

"It's a good thing he didn't succeed or you would have had a lot more to worry about than the missing chip!" declared the supreme judge.

"Yes sir I know how lucky I am," Mannan pulled

a handkerchief from his pants pocket and began wiping the torrent of sweat running from his forehead down across his face. Before he could continue Mr. Phillips stood up and interrupted the process. "Ah, excuse me Supreme Judge, there seems to be a problem, I'm getting a weird reading."

"What do you mean weird? Figure out the problem so we can move on," He ordered.

"It's just a slight variation, either Mr. Mannan is lying or there is a problem with the machine."

"Wha..What?!" Mannan blurted out indignantly, "There must be something wrong with the machine because I can assure you I am not lying!"

"Well Phillips," the supreme judge pushed for an answer, "which is it?"

"Can't be one hundred percent sure sir," Phillips answered while adjusting the knobs on the machine. He then walked over to where Mannan was standing and stopped directly in front of him; just inches away. Peering directly into Mannan's eyes he squinted, his eyes almost disappearing altogether, and went on, "He does seem to be sweating a lot sir, maybe that's interfering with the readings,"

"I noticed that as well. What's with that Mannan, are you hiding something?" the supreme judge asked accusingly.

"No! Of course not! I don't seem to be feeling

quite myself today. Think I might be coming down with something." Mannan reasoned.

"Phillips get out of there we've wasted enough time." The supreme judge said before turning his attention back to Mannan. He was even more shaken at that point and, the longer he stood there, the paler he became. "Pull yourself together and go take a seat. I think I've heard enough."

Next on the stand was an ex co-worker of Justin's, Dawn Casanas. She had worked with Justin up until three years ago when he left the software firm for a better paying job. "She certainly hasn't changed," he thought as he watched her walk over to stand in front of the committee to be sworn in. She wore a short red dress with black stockings and red spike heels. Her hair was piled up on the top of her head and, as usual, she had applied enough makeup for three people. She looked like she was going out on the town not testifying in court. Maybe she thought her attire would give her some favor with the committee.

The supreme judge began his questioning "It is my understanding you worked with Mr. Walker at WorldTech Corporation and during that time you were witness to the accused breaking the law...is that correct."

"Yes, sir." She replied.

"Please present your testimony...and take your time...we don't want you to leave out any important details." He encouraged Dawn gently.

After taking a deep breath, Dawn began recounting the years she had spent with Justin at WorldTech Corp. Justin thought it was pathetically boring but the council seemed to be interested in every minute detail. They leaned forward in their seats engrossed in the picture she was painting. She finally got to her main complaint. Justin remembered the incident in detail.

He had been working on a major account for the VP of the company which had an unrealistic deadline. World Tech Corporation was the global leader for surveillance and responsible for bringing cutting edge surveillance programming for use by the Correctors of Society. Their main technology was a program chip that was surgically implanted into the Corrector's retina. This way the data could be recorded directly into the Global Life History Bank without human contamination. In the early years they relied completely on the testimony of friends, neighbors, and Correctors. However, they found the evidence could easily be tampered with and the statements altered. This new technology made sure that there was no room for dispute; every case was open and shut.

The night before it was due, Justin worked late and finally decided...against strict company law...to take the work home with him in hopes of finishing. His bosses were expecting a presentation first thing in the morning and he needed to make sure it was a success. There wasn't room for failure in this new world; especially in the field of technology.

Justin shook his head in disbelief as she continued her story; she was making it appear worse than it actually was. As if that wasn't bad enough, she then started rattling off a list of petty infractions like being late, missed appointments, or failing to complete projects on time. Assuring the council she understood these things were not enough to judge someone for, she went on to explain how they were prime examples of his continuing disregard for authority. "I'm not surprised to see he finally made it here…just surprised it took so long," she remarked coldly eyeing Justin with contempt.

"Why didn't you report this as soon as it happened?" the Speaker asked.

Dawn, startled at the question, tried her best to recover and give an acceptable answer, "Well, I went to Justin the next day and confronted him about it. He told me he needed to take the information home to complete a special project. He assured me it would never happen again..and well, I did check and found he was telling the truth about the project."

Supreme Judge in a more formal and severe tone answered, "It is very fortunate for you Ms Casanas that you are coming forward with the information now. If we were to have found it out through some other source you may have been appearing before us yourself. Next time I would advise you to leave matters of the law with those empowered to enforce it."

"Of course, I realized the error in my judgment...That's why I'm here today...you are absolutely right...it will never happen again," she stuttered.

"I should hope not. If that is all, you may take your seat," The Supreme Judge dismissed her with a wave of his hand.

As she began to walk away, another thought caused her to stop. "I don't have any proof but one time I saw Justin reading something. I can't say exactly what it was but I've never seen another book like it before."

"Where and when did this happen?" the speaker probed.

"Well, I don't know exactly when, but I remember where. Justin was on his lunch break and went outside to sit in the car. I thought this was weird because he normally ate lunch in his office."

"How did you see him if he was outside in his car," the Speaker asked.

"Like I said, I thought it was suspicious so I went outside to check up on him. He was sitting in his car reading. He was quite startled when I approached him," She explained.

"Did you see what he was reading?" The Supreme Judge asked.

"No, not actually, but I wouldn't be surprised if it was some anti-conformist propaganda. After all, weren't his parents judged for the same thing?" She looked Justin in the eye during her speech like her testimony was payback for not accepting her advances.

"Mr. Phillips!" the Supreme Judge shouted.

"Already on it sir...just one moment. Ahhhh...yes...its right here. In the year 2068 Brian and Joyce Walker were judged for contributing to the corruption of a minor. Justin was ten years old at the time. Numerous books were found on the property and later burned."

"Does it say what exactly they found?"

"Just a brief description...some pre-conformist history...and a book on ancient mythology called the Bible...weird name for a book...never heard of it."

"All right Mr. Phillips...I believe I've heard enough. Ms Casanas please take a seat."

Between the intense pain he was feeling and the stress of the hearing, Justin began to mentally fade away. He sat in the chair, stone faced, eyes facing front while his mind went to a time and place that was much more pleasant.

2
GHOSTS OF THE PAST

Standing in the middle of the family pastures, a ten year old Justin chewed on a blade of grass and waited as two of his friends ran, fishing poles in hand, to meet him. His thoughts were cluttered with wondering what his mom was making for lunch, learning to drive the tractor, and going fishing; nothing of his current circumstances was there to weigh him down.

The memories he had growing up on the family farm outside of Lancaster, Pennsylvania were his best. It was the one time in his life he can remember being truly happy. Once a dairy farm, the property had been transformed into a safe haven for his family. Some of the neighbors followed suit and stood firm on their properties as well, refusing to let the new order contaminate their little piece of the world.

This lifestyle and refusal to conform was enough to make the Committee very unhappy. During the time of great turmoil and as confusion increased, the government pulled people closer into the city limits where they could be better taken care of. Although there weren't any physical barriers put around the cities to keep the residents in, there were the invisible walls of the mind which eventually turned into a prison. Anyone who wanted to leave must have something to hide right? A trip outside of town would immediately put you on the watch list. And, with that, a guaranteed seat in a chair much like Justin's in the near future. These invisible walls were just as effective as those made of stone, barbed wire or steel.

Justin's parents knew their choice wasn't very popular but they didn't care. They were determined to make a life for themselves despite threats from the controllers. And they were doing very well. They had kept a few cows for milk and planted vegetables, fruit trees, grapes and other types of berry bushes. Being self-sufficient and living off of the grid gave them the freedom to live as they wanted. This was something of a rarity these days. Justin's dad made weekly trips to their neighbors to trade milk and produce for oil, gasoline, and other staples. It was a simple life and it suited them all just fine.

The farmhouse sat in the center of fifteen acres. Because they worked it themselves they only cleared the five acres closest to the house. The rest supported a variety of wild life and dense trees and brush. Off to the west side of the property was a small stream, good for fishing and for cooling off during the summer months. When Justin wasn't working the farm with his dad and grandfather, he played in the green fields and swam in the creek that made its way across the property. His dad even tied the old tractor tire on a rope so Justin and his friends from the neighboring farms had a swing that extended out across the deeper end of the creek. They would take turns jumping off into the sparkling ice cold water. When they were exhausted and shivering they would spread out their towels and warm themselves under the summer sun.

Time passed quickly on the farm; there was always something to do in the fields or at the farmhouse. Just about the time Justin developed the perfect tan, the leaves on the big oak outside in the back yard would begin to change colors and drop to the ground. Justin's chores would change from mowing the grass to raking leaves. They saved some for the mulch pile and the rest they burned; Justin loved that smell. The smoke would permeate his hair and everything he was wearing, but he didn't mind. He was never in too much of a hurry to wash it off. Sometimes his mom would have to force him to hand over the smoke saturated clothes and follow up with a nice hot shower. But it was nice while it lasted.

As much as Justin loved the farm in Autumn, there was nothing like it during winter. The nights would begin to get colder and pretty soon Justin's mom would have to drag out the heavy comforters. Most times she would hang them outside before putting one on the bed but no matter what she did, it never seemed to lose that smell of mothballs. Over the years Justin had gotten used to that faint odor and he hardly even noticed anymore.

Just like the falling leaves announced the beginning of fall, the down comforter brought in winter. It wasn't long before the ground began to feel hard under Justin's work boots. Each step he took was followed by a crisp snapping sound. Justin couldn't wait until the first snowfall; some years it was just a light dusting but other years it was knee high. These mornings, Justin would get up extra early so he could get his chores done before lunch. After eating a hurried meal he put on an extra layer of clothing before heading out the door. Grabbing the small wooden sled he would head for the hill behind the farmhouse. Soon afterwards the neighbor kids would join him on the slope. When they got too cold and needed to warm up they would file into the farm house and his mom would make them some of her famous homemade chicken noodle soup and fresh baked bread.

The days on the farm weren't all about work and play, his education was also important. His mother homeschooled him and made sure Justin studied and kept up his grades. She also made sure she exposed Justin to books; not those which had been written after the change, but marvelous works that were now banned. Every night they spent time reading through the books. The Bible, which the family coveted, was read aloud by his father each night. They would sit in the living room in front of the warm glow of the fireplace and listen to the promises of hope that leapt off the pages. On Justin's sixth birthday his mother gave him a small copy of the Bible which he read faithfully. He kept it along with his other precious keepsakes in his secret hiding spot. His parents kept the Bible and the rest of the books under the brick hearth in front of the fireplace. There was a small slot in one of the bricks. His father would insert his pocket knife into the hole and with a slight twist, lift the brick out of the way exposing their literary treasure. They were always careful to make sure the books were put in the hiding spot and the stones replaced to keep their secret well hidden.

Although most of the neighbors were Christians themselves and owned banned Bibles, they never disclosed where the items were kept. However, nothing could keep any one of them from talking about the Lord and encouraging each other in the stand against the new order. They supported each other the best way that they knew how; and that was by sharing the Word and prayer.

This simple lifestyle was out of place in the new age of technology and unification. And, although they weren't forced off their land it was made quite clear the committee wasn't pleased. In fact, the Correctors of Society made numerous trips to their farm as well as the others' farms to try to "convince" them it would be in their best interest to join the others in the safety of the city borders. Every time they would show up on the doorstep of the farm house, his mother would hurry him into his upstairs bedroom and order him to lock the door and not come out. Many times he pressed his ear up against the door to hear what was being said but the old farmhouse doors were solid wood. All he could hear was muffled speech. Once, Justin remembers, his father had a black eye and some scratches on his face but they never spoke about it. And Justin knew this was a topic that was not going to be discussed with him, even if he asked.

His first real experience with the correctors came one summer night when he was around eight years old. His parents went to the Emerson's farm to barter their fresh produce for some kerosene for the lanterns. His grandfather, Bud, was home keeping an eye on him. They had just finished eating dinner and went into the living room to play checkers when there was a knock on the front door. They were both startled at the suddenness of it all. They hadn't heard a sound even though the windows were open to let in the warm summer breeze. Justin didn't have time to run back to his bedroom so he stayed in the living room out of sight while his grandfather went to the door; not before grabbing his shot gun.

He slowly cracked opened the door, the barrel of his shotgun greeting his uninvited guests.

"Now, now, Mr. Walker put the gun down, there's no reason for violence. This is a peaceful visit. "the first corrector feigned a smile as he spoke.

"I'll keep it right where it's at," he replied eyeing the correctors suspiciously, "What do you want?"

"Well, we don't want anything. In fact, we stopped to see if there was anything we could do for you." He continued, the other corrector standing directly behind him.

"We have everything we need here; we don't need anything from you," Bud said slowly and purposefully, holding the rifle up so the opening of the barrel was chest high to the closest corrector.

This didn't make him happy at all. Putting his hand on the barrel of the gun he pushed it to the side aggressively. No one was going to threaten him especially some back woods hick. His face flushed with anger as he moved closer, his words halting and deliberate, "You have no idea what you're doing; threatening me is the biggest mistake you've ever made. Take my advice and put the gun away before we decide to take you in right now."

"This is my property and as I see it, you're

trespassing. I'm just defending what's mine. So, I'd appreciate it right now if you'd please leave before anything bad happens," Bud responded forcefully, not intimidated by the threat.

The enraged corrector took a step towards Bud, fully intending to forcibly remove the gun from his hands and give him a beating with it. The second corrector, grabbed his partner by the back of the shirt stopping him short. "I guess this is a bad time...we'll come back later," he stated before dragging his partner off the porch and shoving him into the awaiting vehicle.

"Don't come back! You won't be so lucky next time!"Bud shouted before firing a shot in the air for affect. Turning around he saw Justin standing behind him in the doorway. "What are you doing out here boy? I told you to stay inside."

Justin had never seen his grandfather so angry before. He didn't bother trying to utter a defense but hurried back inside the home and into the living room. Bud followed locking the front door behind him. He normally kept the gun in the downstairs hall closet but thought it best to leave it beside the front door. Just in case they had any more uninvited visitors to the farm.

"Come on, let's finish our game," Bud coaxed a shaken Justin back to the checkers game. The rest of the evening passed uneventfully and soon it was time for Justin to go to bed. "Good night Pap,"

Justin said hugging him around the neck.

"See ya in the morning boy," Bud replied returning his hug.

Justin was so tired he flopped into bed fully dressed. He didn't hear his parents pull up in the old pickup minutes later, he was fast asleep. In fact he was so tired he didn't wake up when his mother came into the room, pulled off his shoes, and tucked him in.

The next morning Justin woke up early and threw on his clothes. The delicious smell of freshly baked bread drifted up the stairs and into his bedroom. His stomach growled with hunger and anticipation as he ran down the steps and headed for the kitchen. A fresh loaf of warm bread was on the counter cooling. Justin went over to it and inhaled deeply before going over to the table and sitting down. "Good morning Justin, you're up early," his mother greeted him with a smile and a quick kiss on the top of the head.

"Yeah, I'm going out with Pap this morning to check the crops in the west part of the field," Justin explained.

"Well, he took off up the road on the tractor about an hour ago to check on part of the fencing. Your dad noticed a couple of the sections were broken and we can't afford to have any of the cows wandering out again. He said he'd be back to get you after breakfast," she replied, setting a plate of eggs, bacon, and two slices of warm bread slathered with butter in front of him. "Eat up you have a long day ahead of you."

Justin didn't need any coaxing, he was hungry and his mom was an awesome cook.

"Did Pap tell you what happened yesterday," Justin questioned.

"Yes Justin, your dad and I wanted to talk to you about it. We were going to wait until later when he got home." His mother explained.

"Oh, ok, I was just wondering," he said halfheartedly. He couldn't stop thinking about what had happened the night before.

"It's ok Justin, just eat your breakfast and stop worrying," she smiled, giving his shoulder a reassuring squeeze.

Justin quickly polished off his food and then headed outside to wait for his grandfather. The front porch stretched the entire length of the house and afforded a great view of the dirt road his grandfather set out on. Justin, fully expecting him to pull up at any minute, sat on the top step and waited.

Sure enough it was only moments later that he heard the rumble of the old tractor engine. Justin got up slowly and took a few steps toward the sound. He wasn't exactly looking forward to working that morning but always enjoyed the time that he spent with his pap. Justin thought his grandfather was a lot of fun. He also let Justin get away with a lot more than his parents ever did. His pap called it "grandparent's rights". He even let him take a turn around the wheat field in the tractor. His father would say it was a waste of precious gasoline but his pap argued that "a boy needs to have a little fun once in awhile". He was also a fantastic storyteller and would tell Justin stories of his life growing up; it was a completely different world than Justin's and he was fascinated by it.

The engine noise continued to get louder. Soon Justin could see the black exhaust from the tractor floating in the breeze. "Yep, that's him," Justin thought as he got up to stand in the driveway and wait.

He was a little confused at first to see his father behind the wheel of the tractor. His confusion turned to fear when he saw his father's ashen face. Justin turned and ran into the house frantically calling for his mother. He didn't know what happened but he knew it wasn't good. His mom dropped the dish that she was washing, quickly dried off her hands on her apron and returned outside with Justin to see what all the commotion was about.

By that time they came out of the house, Justin's father had parked and turned off the key silencing the old beast. He sat there, key in his hand, head down. A few eternal seconds later he turned to face his family unsure of how to break the news. Justin saw the intense pain in his father's eyes causing him to begin to cry softly. He didn't know what had happened but he knew it wasn't good; something had happened to his grandfather.

His father took a deep breath and began to explain what had happened. He was out working in the vegetable garden when he heard a loud noise that sounded like gunfire. He went up to investigate because sometimes the neighbors wandered onto their property while hunting. While Justin's dad didn't mind, he wanted to make sure they weren't too close to the house. What he found was the tractor a couple of miles up the road stuck in a small ditch; the motor still running. There was no sign of his Pap but signs that something terrible had happened. Justin's eyes immediately went to the small round stains on the side of the tractor. They hadn't been there before. He now recognized them as blood. Unfortunately, there was no sign of Justin's grandfather or what or who had caused his disappearance. But, they didn't need any evidence to know who had been responsible for his disappearance, especially after what happened the day before. His dad searched the entire area and came up with nothing. In fact, he continued to search the area for weeks afterwards before resigning himself to the fact that there wasn't anything to find. During that time Justin was confined to the house. His parents were worried that the controllers would make another visit to the farm and they didn't want Justin in harm's way.

Justin never saw his grandfather again. And after that, his parents became even more cautious and reclusive. They even stopped visiting the neighboring farms except if they needed to trade for supplies. Justin felt like the family farm had turned into the family prison.

Two years later the farm was revisited and the remainder of Justin's family was taken. Justin's memories aren't clear; he vaguely remembers the night. Part of his memory loss could be attributed to the trauma of the event. The other culprit was the eight years of reprogramming that he received at the orphanage.

The last night Justin spent as part of his family only comes to his mind in bits and pieces. He remembers his mother screaming as the doors of the farmhouse were broken down and they were dragged into the living room by gunpoint. He remembers correctors spreading through his home destructively searching for evidence against them. And, the last thing he remembers about his parents is the look on his mother's face as one of the correctors grabbed him by the scruff of the neck and dragged him outside and into a waiting vehicle. That one look said it all; it was the last time he'd ever see her again. His parents were brought out soon afterwards and put in another vehicle; just before the house was set on fire.

3
FIXING THE BROKEN

The small cot rattled with Justin's uncontrolled movements; he couldn't stop shaking. He lay curled in a fetal position, the sharp metal springs pushing through the thin mattress and into his tiny body. Trying his best to become invisible, he grasped the tattered blanket with clenched fists and pulled it over his head.

His parents had told him about the city orphanages and the poor children that were sent there. Besides the stereotypic traits of an orphanage, Greenville Youth Center offered much more; it was also the local reprogramming center. You see, all of the children that were sent there were orphaned the same way, by the government. They had been removed because either one or both parents had been sent to be judged. It didn't matter if you had other relatives or not, you were sent there anyway. The government couldn't take the chance that the child was of the same mind as his or her parents. They sent them all to the orphanage to be reconditioned and molded into perfect little citizens.

Not wanting to infect the rest of the population with the psychosis of free-will and a passion for "something more", these children were tightly guarded, monitored day and night, and underwent extensive therapy to make them "normal". Those who didn't succumb to the brain restructuring process were quickly and quietly judged as soon as they reached their eighteenth birthday. Not wanting to appear barbaric by slaughtering young children, the center found a clean and publically acceptable way around the problem. They were just quietly imprisoned at the orphanage until they were forgotten and the time was right to take care of the problem.

It was in the early hours of the morning that an exhausted Justin fell asleep. His fitful slumber was cut short when a loud alarm sounded precisely at 6:00 am. Twelve other boys ranging in age from six to eleven were also housed In North Hall where Justin slept. He hadn't even noticed them last night when he was brought to the dormitory; he was in shock at being ripped away from his parents and his home. The obnoxious alarm startled him awake and out of bed. He looked around like a scared animal, eyes wide, looking for a way to escape. His heart thudded so hard in his chest he was sure everyone could hear it.

Justin slowly backed himself against the nearest wall and watched the other boys. Like little soldiers, they ran to stand in a straight line in front of the row of beds. They were all in place and standing at attention before the alarm even stopped ringing. It was the strangest thing he had ever seen. The boys appeared to be more machine than human. They silently and motionlessly stood waiting and the normal chatter and light roughhousing one would expect from a group of young boys was absent.

Justin continued to stand there away from the rest of the group. He looked around the room taking in its dilapidated condition. The building was old and the paint around the windows peeling. The walls were dirty and in need of new paint and the furnishings were very sparse; a cot for each boy and a small shelf by each bed for personal belongings. There were bars on the outside of the windows to keep everyone in, or out; it just depended on which side of the bars you were on. Greenville was such a quaint town. The presence of the orphanage was like a scar marring the landscape. The building and grounds were old and neglected while the surrounding neighborhood bright and clean. However, the residents of Greenville wouldn't think of complaining. These types of orphanages were necessary and were established all over the country.

The boys stood there silently until the double wooden doors of the room swung open and a man came walking in. He wore a plain gray suit that looked more like a uniform. He gave little notice to the boys but walked directly to Justin, stopping in front of him.

"Well Justin, I know you're new here so I won't hold you responsible for not knowing the rules." He abruptly grabbed Justin by the front of his t-shirt, dragging him over to the lineup. He shoved him in line between two other boys. They didn't even waver as Justin's small body ran into them; they remained at attention with eyes fixed to some invisible form directly in front of them. Just then the loud speaker crackled before a woman began making the morning announcement. "Place your right hand over your heart and repeat the oath." Voices throughout the orphanage came together as one and echoed through the halls. Justin slowly put his hand to his heart and tried to follow the unfamiliar words.

"I pledge my allegiance and my life to the unity and greatness of the new order.
Alone I am nothing, have nothing, can do nothing. But together with my universal family there is nothing I cannot do.
I will conform to the laws knowing that without unity there is no peace. And I willingly give my life to preserve this unity.
May the government look favorably upon me and give me a full and long life."

Once the pledge was finished the boys broke from their formation and began to tidy their beds.

Justin once again began receiving instruction from the unnamed man. "Tomorrow you will be in another ward with all of our new arrivals. You will wake up exactly at 6:00 am every morning and line up for the daily oath and inspection with the other wards. After that you will brush your teeth and dress before coming down to the dining hall for breakfast. I don't want to have to tell you this again. Do you understand?"

"Yes sir" Justin half whispered.

"Breakfast is in exactly..um," looking down at watch, " fifteen minutes. Don't be late." And he abruptly walked out of the room. The doors slammed behind him echoing loudly through the sparse room.

Justin didn't know where he was supposed to go or what he was supposed to do so he threw on his clothes and followed the boys out of the room, in single file. They went down a long wooden staircase to the front hall. It was enormous! It seemed like it went on forever. The hallway was extremely wide and sparsely decorated like the rest of the place. The doors to the common room were propped open with wooden doorstops and Justin could see some of the other children already seated at the long tables inside. A rough wood sign with the words "Dining Hall" carved in it hung above the entryway. As they entered the room they picked up a tray off the table located along the left side of the wall. Then, after getting a tray, the boys walked down the food line to the right and their breakfast was scooped up and plopped onto the tray by cafeteria workers. There was no "good morning" or even a friendly smile or nod to be had in the place. They barely noticed him as he moved his tray through the line.

Justin looked down disdainfully at the serving that lay sloshing out of the individualized compartment on his tray. The runny eggs didn't look anything like the light fluffy ones he was used to eating. There were two slices of bacon, can't do much wrong to bacon, a slice of toast and a glass of room temperature water. The meal was not very appetizing, even for a hungry boy.

Justin sat at the first empty table he passed and stared down at his breakfast. He picked up the fork but instead of using it to eat, he half-heartedly pushed his food around. It wasn't long before he saw a shadow appear over his shoulder and then a large man's hand clasped it tightly.

"Listen to me boy," came the impatient voice of the guardian. Justin sat unmoving while he was spoken to. "In this orphanage we are grateful for the food our government has provided. We don't waste anything. Pick up your fork and start eating now! You have ten minutes before your orientation and you better be finished."

"I'm not hungry sir," Justin mumbled quietly.

The words were barely out of his mouth before his head was launched forward by the forceful slap of the guardian's hand. "I'm not asking you; It's an order. If you refuse to obey an order, whether it comes from me or any other authority, you will be punished severely. How hungry are you now boy?"

Justin, at first shocked by the blow, immediately picked up his fork and began shoving eggs in his mouth.

"Don't forget to drink your water," the guardian added before walking away, "all of it."

Justin quickly complied and finished off the awful meal and bitter tasting water before the next bell rang. Before he had time to wonder what to do next, the loud speaker crackled alive with static and the woman he heard earlier that morning began to speak again." All new arrivals to Greenville report directly to room 453 in the main hall."

"Well that's me," he thought. Justin returned his tray and then reluctantly made his way down the hall looking for the room. The passage had once been painted a bright blue but had since faded and begun to peel like everything else. The building had settled over the years leaving large cracks that ran from the ceiling to the corners of the each of the door jambs. The door numbers themselves had long since worn off and someone had hand painted their replacements; and not very well. It was obvious that very little importance was placed on Greenville's appearance and upkeep. Justin thought it reminded him more of camp than a home for children. Even the old outhouse that pap built out in the field was kept in better shape than this.

It only took him a few minutes to find the right room down at the very end of the hall. When he opened the door and went inside he was surprised to see four other children already there. There was a young girl who appeared to be around five year's old sitting in the chair closest to the door. She had short tufts of blond curls all over her small head. Her large blue eyes looked at him expectantly. He couldn't help but smile at her, she was so cute. She sported a slightly skewed self stick name tag that read "Jennifer". Another boy named Peter sat directly behind her. When Justin entered he looked at him with an expression of relief. Apparently, when Justin opened the door, Peter thought it was someone else. He had sandy brown hair and freckles and, despite their situation, a smile crinkled up the corners of his mouth in greeting. Justin later found out that Peter was only months younger than him and came from a background similar to his own. In fact, they had so much in common they quickly became close friends. An older boy of around 16 years of age stood in the back, arms folded across his chest. His paper name tag lay on the seat in front of him.   It was upside down but Justin could make out the name "Daniel" printed on it. He almost looked like a thug standing there with his black crew cut and muscular build but the fleeting glimpse of fear Justin saw in his eyes proved otherwise. And then there was Carrie. Carrie sat in the far corner of the room. Slightly younger than Justin, she was a quiet girl with long red hair and porcelain skin.   Justin thought she looked as if she could have stepped right out of the glass front display cabinet at the farmhouse which held his mom's doll collection. She had deep grey piercing eyes that shined with spirit and intelligence.   Justin was mesmerized by her appearance and found it difficult to move his eyes past her.

Before they had time for formal introductions, the door opened and a guardian stepped into the room. Justin quickly picked up his own name tag from the small table by the door and took a seat with the rest of the kids. He peeled it off and stuck it to his shirt. The man didn't speak immediately causing the children to become anxious. He looked at each of them directly for several seconds as if assessing them. They sat there in silence, the air thick with trepidation, waiting. When he finally did speak, it was evident everything they had known and loved was gone. When they crossed the threshold of Greenville, they had died to their old lives and woke up in hell.

While pacing across the front of the room, the man began to speak slowly, "I am Number 639 and I will be in charge of you during your stay at Greenville. "

Jennifer giggled, clasping a small chubby hand over her mouth trying to hide the escaping sounds. 639 stopped in front of her and asked impatiently, "What is so funny?"

"Your name is 639? That's a number not a name," Jennifer answered merrily, still unaware that 639 was getting irritated with her.

"My name is not 639 but that is what you will call me. I do not like you; I am not your friend, your brother, your uncle or your father. I do not want a relationship with you of any kind. I do not care about you, you are my job, nothing more," he ranted angrily, "and that is why you will call me 639. Understand?" As he glanced around the room, his eyes were as cold as the words he spoke.

Jennifer looked at him silently and nodded her head in understanding. The others sat there just as quiet not wanting to draw any attention to themselves.

"Do you know why you're here?" Looking around at the terrified faces he continued without waiting for an answer. "You're here because your parents were criminals. Your parents didn't care about you. They broke laws and would have harmed you if we didn't step in and do something. In fact, you could say we saved your lives." His eyes full of disgust, he stopped his pacing long enough to reach out and brush the wispy bangs of young Jennifer out of her eyes. She sat quietly, looking up at him confused with the whole situation. At the touch of his fingers she cringed slightly edging away from him, still shaken by the previous tirade. He smiled, no sneered at her before turning away.

"My mommy's not bad," Jennifer whispered barely audible in defense. Number 639 stopped dead in his tracks and spun on his heels to abruptly face her. He bent down so her eyes were level with his own. None too gently he grasped her chin with thumb and two fingers while he continued talking.

"So much trouble for such a little girl." It came out almost a growl. "I've about had all I care to take from you. Here in the orphanage there are strict rules. The number one rule is not to question anything I say. I only speak the truth. If I say your parents are criminals then they are criminals." He quickly let go of her trembling chin, stood and resumed walking the parameter of the small room.

Jennifer bit her lower lip and her eyes filled with tears. The red marks left by his grasp lingered. Justin sat there like the rest too terrified to speak up. Peter's face drained of color, Carrie sat staring at her lap, and Daniel returned 639's look defiantly.

He appeared not to notice, still focused on finishing the orientation.

"There is a price associated with everything you do. If you do well you will be rewarded. On the other hand, if you are disobedient, you will be punished. I don't want to punish you but when you don't obey you force my hand. It is for your own good, to make you great citizens of the new order." He stopped walking directly in front of Daniel and looked at him intently. Daniel stood his ground for several long seconds before he too succumbed to the intimidation. He quickly averted his eyes downward and slumped into the nearest chair.

"These rules were made so this great establishment can continue to run smoothly and to give you what you need. That way, someday you can leave here and join the rest of society. How pleasant your stay is and what type of future you have is entirely up to you."

"We're done for now." He said abruptly. He looked into the camera hanging in the upper corner of the room and motioned with his head. Seconds later the door opened and a woman entered. She was dressed in a gray uniform as well but also wore cap which was pulled down over short severely styled brown hair. She ushered the children out of the room and into their classes which were already in progress.

After class the woman in gray, later identified as

Matron 85, took Justin and the other children to their new quarters in the far upper west tower. Here they were isolated from the rest of the children. They would continue to have separate rooms until deemed fit to join the general population. Jennifer and Carrie shared a small room at one end of the tower and the three boys shared a room at the opposite end. They each had a cot with a thin mattress and one blanket and pillow. Toiletries were also provided but were only replaced on a monthly basis. If you got too zealous with the soap or toothpaste you might have to go a few days or even weeks without a proper shower and tooth brushing. Matron 85 occupied a room on the same floor halfway between that of the boys and girls. A perfect spot to see everything on that floor.

The only time they were allowed to talk amongst themselves was during meal times and in the short time it took them to go to or come from daily calisthenics.

Health was also a requirement of the new age. Since healthcare was provided by the government, one was expected to maintain good health. The government didn't want to waste precious money on people who were insensitive enough not to take care of themselves. Mass produced unhealthy food choices were a thing of the past. Now, the government made all of the food choices for you.

Nice and easy, nothing to worry about. And, if you were one of the unfortunate few that developed some disease or cancer, you were admitted to the hospital. But, it was unlikely you would ever leave. The laws and the beliefs of the new order had been so engrained in the thinking of the masses that no one even complained or thought twice about the untimely death of a loved one. Or, if they did, they weren't about to admit it to anyone else. To keep disease at bay, every man, woman, and child participated in some sort of physical fitness routine and those at the orphanage were not exempt.

Each child was ushered out into the courtyard at the back of the building and expected to participate in the stretching and muscle building exercises. Once calisthenics was over, the children filed in for dinner and then it was time to go back to their rooms and read new-world history or do homework. Or, if you were Daniel, it was a time to plan an escape. During this time light music and new order ideals played over the loudspeakers. At first Justin found it a distraction but soon, he hardly even noticed it.

Before bed, Matron 85 brought them a nice cup of hot milk to help them sleep and then it was lights out at 8:00 p.m. The last thought Justin had before he slipped into the peacefulness of slumber was that he might be coming down with something because he didn't feel quite himself. The next thing he knew, the bell was ringing and it was time to do it all over again.

The second day the kids were introduced to the doctor who would be overseeing their therapy. It was required, because of what they had been exposed to, that they each undergo behavior modification treatments with Doctor X. Doctor X was a tiny Asian woman with striking features. The only thing that stopped her from being beautiful was the lack of humanity she showed. She was devoid of any human emotion and didn't like it when anyone else appeared to have any. Even on the rare times she did smile, it never reached her eyes. They remained large dark portals into a scary and twisted mind. At first the sessions were non-threatening discussions about childhood memories and personal history. After the doctor felt a child was beginning to open up, she used numerous techniques, including chemical brainwashing and memory suppression, to ensure he or she could be molded into something new; something they felt was better. In most cases the child didn't even realize what was happening.

Those more resistant to the treatments were subjected to electrical shock therapy and other extreme therapy methods. Fortunately, most of the children were young enough and pliable enough to avoid radical treatment. However, there some like Daniel whose rebellious nature ensured them not only shock therapy but also time in the "black box".

The first week Daniel spent miserable and frustrated. He didn't even bother to try to hide his feelings from anyone. He spent hours peering through the barred windows in his bedroom. At first Justin and Daniel tried to pull him into their conversations but when Daniel didn't want to talk they found it was usually best to leave him alone. The two boys often talked about family and the life they once lived, sharing funny family memories that usually ended up with one of them in tears. They also spent a lot of time talking about what they would do once they were released from the orphanage. Their plans included doing anything and everything they could to shut down the orphanages. Daniel usually expressed his cynicism with a scoff or some unrecognizable words spoken under his breath. Justin and Peter never got mad at him though; they knew he was hurting too.

Sometimes late at night, after they were given their warm milk and lights out, Daniel would slide silently out of his bed and onto the floor. From there he would make his way over to the bedroom door and crack it open slightly. He had a great view of the hall and most importantly Matron 85's bedroom. Besides having the Matron as a watchdog, there was a camera at the far end of the hall near the girls' room. He checked it out that morning on the way down to breakfast. It was an old one, very old, and pretty dirty. Even though Daniel only had seconds to glance at it as he passed, he was able to see it was in poor condition. He wondered if it even worked. For all they knew it was just there for show.

One night several weeks into their stay at the orphanage Daniel decided to see just how good the camera worked. He sat, one eye peering out of the crack in the door waiting for matron's bedroom light to go out. He didn't leave at that moment but stayed there for another hour to make sure she was fast asleep. Then, without waking up the other boys, he slowly opened the door just enough to slide his body through. Standing there sweating, Daniel waited for the alarms and Matron 85 to come running down the hall. After several minutes, that felt like hours, nothing happened and he was able to breathe normally again. The hall was long and narrow with four very narrow windows on either side of the passageway. Fortunately the sky was overcast so only a few stray rays of moonlight shown through the dirty panes. Daniel placed each step strategically, staying in the darkest of the shadows. When he reached Matron's room he stopped. Her door was open but it was so dark he could barely make out her form lying on the bed. He was convinced she was sleeping though; her snores could have waked the dead. He began the other half of his journey more confident.   Either he was right and the camera was broke or it was so dark and the camera so old, that it couldn't pick him up. Reaching the girls' room, he tapped lightly on the door and whispered Carrie's name. Several seconds later the door cracked open and Jennifer stood there looking up at Daniel shocked.

"How did you get here?" she whispered. Daniel put his finger up to his lips before gently pushing past her and into the bedroom.

"Daniel!" Carrie exclaimed sitting upright in bed and pulled the coverlet up to her chin. She was a little startled because the sound of their voices had pulled her out of a deep sleep.

"Shhh, guys you are gonna get me caught," Daniel admonished, "It's easy but you gotta be quiet. Come with me."

"I don't know…,"Carrie started.

"Come on Carrie the witch is sleeping, there's nothing to be afraid of."

"What about the camera?" she added.

"If that worked right I wouldn't have even made it to your room, you know that. Come on you guys trust me, ok?"

"Ok, Daniel, I guess," Carrie finally resigned. She put the thin blanket around her shoulders like a shawl and then took Jennifer by the hand. They followed Daniel closely down the dark hallway. She was so nervous that even her breathing sounded loud enough to get them caught. Jennifer must have been just as scared because her tiny hand was sweaty and clinching her own so tightly it was cutting off the circulation. They were all relieved when they slipped safely into the boys' room and closed the door behind them.

"Whew," Carrie said before sitting on the floor, her legs were shaky from the journey down the hall. She pulled Jennifer to sit next her on the floor, her hand still clutching her tightly. Justin and Peter were now awake too and joined them on the floor. Justin made sure he took the opening nearest Carrie.

"I can't believe you guys did this," Peter said in a very worried tone, "we're going to get in a lot of trouble if they catch us."

"Yeah, *if* they catch us," Daniel retorted, "which they're not."

"Ok, don't argue, we don't have a lot of time," said Justin playing the peacemaker.

"I wonder why they didn't see us," Carrie questioned, "there's a camera at the end of the hall."

"It looks a lot older than the ones downstairs plus it's really dark up here," Daniel reasoned.

"Whatever the reason," Justin interjected, "I'm just glad we can talk without being watched."

The others agreed and spent several hours

talking about their experiences so far at the orphanage. Daniel was encouraged by the fact they were able to move around undetected. If he could accomplish this maybe there was a way out! Now that they had a way to get together without anyone knowing, they made a pact to meet several times through the week. It seemed like the night passed quickly and it was time for Jennifer and Carrie to get back to their rooms before the alarm brought in another day. They quietly made their way back to the room just as they had left it only hours earlier. As they passed Matron 85's room, Carrie noticed that something was different this time. It was too quiet!

"I don't hear her snoring", Carries whispered panicking. Jennifer let out a little moan and Carrie could feel her body shaking as it got closer to her own. Carrie grabbed Jennifer's hand and rushed towards their room. Jennifer could barely keep on her feet. Once they crossed the threshold of the room Carrie shoved Jennifer towards her bed and jumped into her own. She barely had time to pull up the blanket and close her eyes before Matron 85 was in the room and flicked on the light switch.

4
A SHOT AT FREEDOM

Daniel, Justin and Peter held their breath as they watched Matron enter the girl's bedroom and close the door firmly. All they could hear was the muffled speech of first Matron and then each of the girls. The room was too far away and the doors too solid to hear much else. They sat there peeking out of the crack in the door waiting. Almost an hour later Matron came out and returned to her own room. As soon as they saw her they shut their door and scrambled into bed. The boys were anxious to find out what happened but not enough to try to venture out of the bedroom again. Every worst case scenario played through their young minds. They spent half the night talking about all the "what ifs?" and worrying if they were going to be visited too.

The next morning the boys, albeit exhausted, managed to get ready, dress, and make their way downstairs before the girls. Justin had just placed his tray on the table and began to sit with the other two, when Carrie and Jennifer walked into the room. Carrie met their anxious looks with a smirk and a wink before getting in line for breakfast, Jennifer as always was in tow. After picking up their trays of food they went over to the boy's table and joined them for breakfast.

"I should get an award for my acting performance last night, thank you very much," Carrie joked and bowed slightly before sitting next to Justin. "And Jennifer, she was a natural with those big innocent eyes; Matron didn't suspect a thing. In fact, she was actually kinda apologetic for waking us up."

"Yeah, she fixed my blankets for me too, she never does that," added Jennifer.

"What took her so long, she was in there forever," Justin questioned.

"She didn't seem to be in a big hurry to leave. After making sure we were settled in bed, she stayed and waited for us to fall asleep. Of course we faked it. Who could fall asleep with her watching," Carrie explained.

"Old witch," Daniel muttered and chuckled. "Witch" had become Daniel's pet name for Matron, at least behind her back. One of these days, Carrie warned him, he was going to slip up and say it to her face.

"I think we need to play it cool for a couple of days just in case," Peter suggested.

"Yeah, Peter's right. Justin agreed, "We don't want to mess up a good thing".

"Ok, that's fine with me," Carrie stated, "I almost had a heart-attack last night...I could use a night or two before we try it again."

"Alright then, we meet in our room in two

nights. Just make sure you wait long enough for Matron to fall asleep." Daniel instructed.

"Oh don't worry, I'll make sure she's sleeping before I try anything again," Carrie re-assured Daniel solemnly.

The bell rang and once again the five friends split up to go to their classes. The rest of the day was uneventful and they began to relax in the realization that they had outsmarted Matron and the others. Two nights later, just as planned, Carrie and Jennifer made their way to the boys' room. Jennifer thought Matron must have been extremely tired because her snores echoed louder than usual through the dark hallway. Staying in the shadows as they did in their previous trip, they came to the door to the boy's room without mishap.

Once inside, the group sat huddled together on the floor eager to talk about their day.

"Had my first meeting with the doc today," Peter whispered to the group.

"Oh, no!" Carrie said sympathetically, "what happened?"

"Not much, she just kept asking me questions about my family and stuff, nothing important." Peter dismissed the incident with a shrug of his shoulders.

"That's just how it starts," Daniel warned, "be careful."

"I know, I'm not stupid," Peter replied defensively.

"I have mine tomorrow," Justin jumped in.

"Me too," Jennifer's small voice interjected on the tail of Justin's words.

"Don't worry Jennifer, It will be ok," Carrie scooted closer and gave her a reassuring hug.

"The doc seems nice at first, like she wants to be your friend," Daniel explained, "Don't believe it, it's just a trick."

"How do you know Daniel?" Carrie questioned in disbelief.

"I just do, ok?" Daniel offered reluctantly.

"Come on Daniel, what's going on?" Justin pushed.

"It's just I've been seeing the doc since we first got here," Daniel confessed.

"What?" Carrie admonished, "why didn't you say anything?"

"I didn't want you to think I was brain washed or anything," Daniel replied softly, head down.

"Don't be silly," Carry responded giving him a playful slap, "you're the last person that we think is brainwashed. In fact, I don't think they could brain wash you if they tried!"

"Yeah, come on Daniel," Justin joined in agreement with Carrie, "You should know better than that."

"You're our friend," Peter added, "you can tell

us anything."

"Ok, ok, I get it," Daniel chuckled, "I won't let it happen again."

"Better not," Jennifer said in her best stern voice, hands on her small hips. This was enough to send them into a fit of laughter. When they were all laughed out, they decided it was a good place to end the night. Saying their goodbyes, Carrie and Jennifer made their way back to their own bedroom. This time Matron stayed fast asleep. Carrie tucked Jennifer into bed and told her a bedtime story, one about a beautiful princess that had been locked away in a dungeon. Of course there was a handsome prince to rescue her and slay the evil beast that put her there. It reminded Carrie of their stay at the orphanage. They had been locked away and they were just waiting for someone to rescue them. Unfortunately they lived in the real world and no one was going to burst in riding on a white horse to save them. She sighed and lay back on her bed and stared through the dark at the ceiling. It wasn't long before she fell into a restless sleep and dreamt about being chased by monsters.

Carrie woke up with a feeling of dread, the uneasiness of the dream following her. She slowly stretched and tried to collect her thoughts before getting up. Jennifer was already awake and getting dressed. Seeing that her roommate was awake,

Jennifer pounced on her bed and gave her a good morning hug. Carrie looked forward to that bit of affection every day. She brushed Jennifer's bangs back and peered into her eyes trying to gauge how she was doing. It was obvious that she was upset however she denied it profusely. After the morning announcements and pledge, Carrie brushed out Jennifer's hair and pulled it back into pigtails. When she was sure her little ward was ready, she hurriedly donned her clothes and quickly brushed her teeth and own hair. Even though she always made sure to take care of Jennifer first, Carrie managed never to be downstairs late; today was no different.

The heaviness Carrie felt seemed to carry over to the rest of the group. When breakfast was over none of them wanted to go their separate ways. It was like each one of them, for whatever reason, needed to remain in that comforting cocoon of friendship a little longer. Their gazes held fast for a few seconds more before they were pushed onward by Matron and the connection severed.

By the time they made it back to their rooms that evening Jennifer was exhausted. Carrie didn't even have time to tell her a bedtime story before she was fast asleep. She didn't say anything about her visit with the doc and Carrie didn't push it. Jennifer told her everything so it was just a matter of time before she talked about this as well.

Besides, Carrie had other things on her mind. She sat on her own bed and pulled the crumpled paper from her pants pocket. She then opened it smoothing it across her lap. Matron had given it to her after lunch period; it was a reminder to show up at the doc's the next morning. Carrie abruptly wiped the tears now streaming down her face with the back of her hand. It wasn't like she didn't know her turn would be coming soon. And for as much as she scolded herself for being upset, it didn't seem to help the way she felt. She wished she could talk to Justin; he had quickly become her best friend and confidant. Unfortunately, they weren't going to be any nightly visits until later in the week.

The new day didn't bring a change in their mood. If anything, it changed for the worse. They had fought the good fight but they were all starting to get a battle weary. Something was about to change, they could all feel it coming. Unfortunately, they knew that "something" probably wasn't good and there was nothing they could do about it.

They arrived for breakfast as usual but this morning there was no excited chatter or joking around. Carrie didn't even have the emotional energy to tell Justin about her visit to the doc later that morning. Each of them sat quietly eating their mediocre breakfast, lost in their own troubles until the bell rang and the day began.

Three nights later they had another meeting, this time in the girls' room. Everyone seemed a little out of sorts, especially Daniel. He was really getting frustrated and always seemed angry. He wanted out and he didn't care how it happened.

On the other hand, Jennifer was really quiet again tonight. Carrie was really starting to worry about her; lately she was exhausted and emotionally disconnected. In fact, she had barely spoken to Carrie in days. When she did it was only because Carrie wouldn't back off until she got a response.

Peter looked as if he If had been crying earlier; eyes red and swollen. Of course when Justin asked him about it he insisted he wasn't. Justin had become overly nervous and tonight he was obsessing about getting caught. He kept looking out the door like he expected someone to come running down the hall at any minute. And Carrie, everything seemed to be making her cry. The entire group of friends was teetering on the precipice of desperation; they needed something to hope in, and soon.

Just after getting in the room and settling on the floor so they could talk, Daniel went on a rant about how they needed to escape. They were all getting a little tired of it by now.

"Daniel we've heard this all before," Justin

argued.

"Yeah, so what are we going to do," Daniel argued back, "just sit here and talk and never do anything?"

"What can we do," asked Peter "there isn't a way to get out, if there were someone else would have done it before."

"Can't you be positive about anything" Daniel retorted angrily, "this is an old place there has to be a way, we just need to look."

"Hey Daniel, we're on your side," Carrie intervened, "you don't have to be so mean."

"Ok everyone, calm down, you're getting too loud," Justin peered out the door again, "What do you have in mind Daniel?"

"Well, if we got past the camera on this floor maybe we can make it downstairs," Daniel explained.

"Then what?" Peter asked unconvinced that Daniel's plan would work.

"I don't know, maybe get through a window or find a way out of the basement," Daniel went on with more confidence since he had their attention, "They wouldn't think anyone would try so maybe the security isn't that great down there."

"It wouldn't be safe," Jennifer said quietly. All eyes turned on her and Carrie said reassuringly, "Don't worry honey; we won't let anything happen to you." Noticing how sleepy Jennifer looked Carrie suggested they call it quits for the night.

"Daniel, if you think of something, I'm in with you," Peter said unexpectedly, "I don't want to stay here either."

"None of us do Peter," Daniel said passionately, "if there is a way out of this place I'll find it, I promise." He gave Peter's shoulder a soft punch to reassure him that everything was alright between the two of them. After saying their goodbyes, the boys quietly left the room and headed back to their own. In single file, they wove through the shadows lining the hallway until they made it to the destination safely.

Carrie helped Jennifer into her bed and tucked her in. Once again there was no bedtime story. In fact, Jennifer didn't even bother to say goodnight. She just rolled over, back to Carrie, and fell asleep.

It took Daniel awhile to settle himself enough to fall asleep. He climbed into the top bunk above Justin's and flopped down shaking the entire bed. Justin muttered something indistinct but was too tired to get into it with him. Besides, he didn't want to get Daniel started talking again or none of them would get any sleep.

Daniel had a one-track mind set on freedom. He made a promise to his friends and was determined to follow through with it. If there was a way out of this place, he was going to find it.

One morning several weeks later, Jennifer

surprised Carrie by getting ready by herself before Carrie was even awake.

"Good morning sweetie, you must have been up early" Carrie greeted her young friend as she lay in her bed and stretched. Jennifer turned and gave her a slight smile that seemed more perfunctory than sincere.

Carrie sat up on the bed, threw off the bedspread and turned to dangle her legs over the side. "What's wrong Jennifer," Carrie asked softly.

"Nothing..." Jennifer replied and then turned to finish brushing her hair.

Carrie got up and went over and reached out her hand to take the brush. "Here, let me," Carrie offered.

"That's ok, I'm getting big enough to brush my own hair, "Jennifer replied and continued.

"Oh, ok, If you need help just let me know," Carrie said before turning and gathering up her clothes for the day. He eyes welled with tears that she didn't want Jennifer to see. This wasn't like Jennifer and Carrie wasn't exactly sure what to do. Feeling at a loss for what to do, she finished getting dressed in silence and headed down for breakfast right after the pledge.

Although Jennifer continued to eat with her friends, it was obvious something was different. She had lost her playful nature and avoided any displays of affection from her friends. Carrie wasn't sure if the rest of them noticed but she was very aware of the unusual behavior that Jennifer was displaying. She hoped it was just some sort of faze she was going through but doubted it.

Daniel was focused on planning an escape and Peter and Justin were making sure he didn't do anything that would get him into trouble. It was a full time job but their tag-team efforts seemed to work. Carrie left Daniel under the watchful eyes of Peter and Justin while she tried to keep an eye of Jennifer. As time went on, it continued to get worse. Over the next two months Jennifer had completely withdrawn from her friendship with Carrie. Everything that Jennifer had once loved stopped. There were no more bedtime stories, songs, or girl talk. The spirit that had made her eyes twinkle when she laughed and fill with compassion towards her friends was gone. It was like a switch had been turned off.

Carrie tried to think of every reason Jennifer could be acting like that. She tried every reason to justify or excuse Jennifer's behavior. Then, after a conversation with Jennifer one morning, she knew she couldn't avoid the truth any longer.

"Jennifer honey is something wrong?" Carrie asked her gently.

"No," Jennifer whispered refusing to look Carrie directly in the eyes.

"Do you feel all right? Are you sick?" Carrie

prodded.

"No, I'm fine, Carrie," she insisted a little more forcefully. Carrie didn't believe a word she was saying but she couldn't force her to open up and tell her what was going on. However, she wasn't going to let the matter drop. "Jennifer, are you happy here?" Carrie continued.

"It's not so bad I guess," she responded automatically.

Carrie was shocked and sat silent for a second. She couldn't believe what she was hearing. "You mean you like it here? Even after all the bad things they did to us?" she said in astonishment.

"Well they're not all that mean, in fact some of them are nice to me," Jennifer argued.

"It's just a trick Jennifer, you have to know that." Carrie tried to reason with her young friend. "Remember they took you away from your mommy and daddy?"

"I guess…"Jennifer said ending the conversation. She got up and ran out the door and down the stairs to the dining hall and breakfast. It was the first time she had gone without Carrie. Carrie immediately felt sick to her stomach. She knew that she had totally lost her grip on Jennifer; she was now in the clutches of the orphanage.

By the time she made it down to breakfast Jennifer had taken a seat with several other girls her own age at the opposite end of the room.

Carrie grabbed her tray of food and sat down with the boys. "I'm worried about Jennifer she doesn't seem to be herself. "

"Yeah, what's going on? Why is she sitting over there?" Peter asked.

"That's what I mean, she hasn't been acting right lately." Carrie replied. And then she filled them in on the conversation they had prior to breakfast.

"We have to be careful, we can't trust her anymore." Daniel warned.

"What do you mean Daniel? She's one of us!" Carrie argued, the tears threatening to return.

"Carrie, we care about her too but Daniel's right. We don't know what she'll do," Justin tried to reason with her gently, "What if she tells on us?"

"What are we going to do for her? How can we stop it?" Carrie questioned them passionately.

"The only way is to get out of here. None of us are safe if we don't leave," Daniel whispered across the table. "It has to be soon or we will all be just like Jennifer."

Peter's face drained of color and Carrie was trying desperately to hide her tears and not attract attention.

"I got something I better tell you then too," Peter said hesitantly. "I saw Jennifer in the office last week with 639 and Matron 85."

"What! Why didn't you tell us this before?"

Daniel exclaimed angrily. His voice had begun to rise and the matron at the door gave him a look of warning. He shook his head in acknowledgement and they continued their conversation, this time much quieter and less animated.

"Wasn't sure if it meant anything," Peter began, his eyes focused intently on the watery eggs on his tray, "Well..I was hoping it didn't mean nothing."

"Everything means something Peter!" Daniel exclaimed, his voice rising again. The matron at the door held up two fingers. One more time and he would be punished.

Seeing that Daniel's behavior was not only getting him into trouble but making matters worse with Peter, Justin jumped into the conversation. "It's ok Peter, just tell us what happened," Justin coaxed.

Peter looked back up into the waiting faces of his friends. His voice cracked with emotion as he laid out the scene before them. It was Monday morning when he was on his way to first period. The office door was partially opened and he glanced in as he passed. Astonished, he stopped when he saw Jennifer talking with 639 and Matron.

"What were they talking about," questioned Daniel.

"I don't know, couldn't hear," Peter explained. "I got closer to the door but that's when 639 saw me."

"Oh no, what he do?" asked Carrie, scared for her friend.

"He just walked over and slammed the door in my face. I thought I'd get in trouble but he never said anything else," explained Peter. "I figured it was nothing important."

"But it is," Daniel said shortly, "We can't trust anyone or anything in this place. We are all we got." His voiced softened towards the end. They were all each other had; that was a sobering comment. It caused Daniel to ease up on Peter.

"Well, we can't meet anymore because we can't take the chance she'll tell on us." Justin said slowly.

"You're right about that. I'm going to keep looking for a way out. When I figure something out, I'll get a message to you Carrie." Daniel promised. "Other than that, we gotta stay out of trouble. Just act like nothing is wrong." They all agreed this was the best approach to take.

True to their promise to each other, it was as if nothing had ever happened. They continued to treat Jennifer like they always had and loved her even when it was obvious it was the last thing she wanted from them. Carrie continued to hope deep down in her heart that there was still a way to get her Jennifer back. However, everything she tried was futile.

Daniel turned out to make serious efforts

towards getting them out of there. It only took him two weeks of searching before he stumbled on what seemed to be the answer to their prayers. One day after Global History class, the instructor picked Daniel and another boy, Trey, to carry books to the supply closet and re-organize the mess. They quickly restacked some of the larger boxes to make room for the new inventory on the shelving unit. As they were putting the books on the shelf, the edge gave way sending the books to the floor.

"I'll pick them up. You get something to fix this stupid shelf." Daniel instructed before turning and picking up the heavy books. Trey left to find the teacher and get a hammer and nails.

"Of course," Daniel muttered to himself when he saw one of the books had become wedged behind one of the boxes. He got the small dolly from the front of the room, slid it under the box, and moved it a few inches away from the wall. When he bent down to pick up the book he saw a large square heating register cover. The registers used to carry heat from room to room before the new heating system was installed. Daniel quickly inspected it and saw that the screws had been rusted and the register cover was loose. And it was big, big enough for any one of them to crawl through. Just then Trey returned with the items they needed to fix the shelf. Daniel retrieved the fallen book, stood up, and scooted the box in front of the register again, hiding it from sight. He was so excited by the time he returned to the dorm Justin knew something was up just by the look on his face.

"You guys are never gonna believe what I found today," Daniel baited, a wide grin on his face. Before either of them could respond he added, "a way out!"

"What do you mean a way out Daniel," Peter questioned excitedly.

"Yeah, what did you find?" Justin added.

Daniel told them about the register and began to formulate a plan that very night. If he could just sneak down the stairs and into the supply room he could follow it to the basement. The basement was never used for anything more than storage. He had peaked through the dirty windows several times on the way back from daily exercises. If he could make his way down there he could easily break out one of the windows. There were no bars, no cameras, and no alarms. The courtyard was fairly easy to navigate without being detected and there were so many holes in the crumbling stone fence they could effortlessly slip through. The next day between classes Daniel grabbed Justin and shoved him into the empty supply room. He pulled the boxes away from the wall to expose his prize.

"Look, I've already taken the screws out and it's

big enough for us to crawl through," Daniel whispered excitedly.

"I don't know," Justin questioned warily "Where does it go? How are we going to get down here?"

"I think it goes to the basement but I'm not sure. I need to find out though," Daniel said, "I want to sneak down here tonight and try. We gotta do it soon or it won't work. Someone's going to find this."

"Ok, we'll talk about it more tonight. We gotta get to class before they miss us," Justin reasoned, "Come on."

Justin saw Carrie in the hall and told her of the scheduled meeting that night. As a precaution, she waited until Jennifer was fast asleep before leaving to join the boys. They weren't sure how far they could trust her and it was better not to take any chances.

Daniel was a little discouraged at the reaction he received from the rest of the group when he laid out his brilliant plan. He figured they would be as excited as he was.

Peter was the first one to voice his objections, "Even if you make it downstairs, you don't know where the vent even leads. It could just drop off somewhere or go straight into the old furnace!"

"I don't think that's a good idea Daniel, you're going to get yourself killed." Carrie argued, her voice quivered with concern.

"But I have to try," he continued to plead his case, "This is our only hope of getting out of here."

"Maybe there isn't any getting out of here," Peter said quietly, his head down.

"I can't believe that," Daniel said passionately, his eyes bright with unshed tears. "I refuse to believe it!"

Justin continued, "Daniel, we all want to get out of here but it's not worth you getting hurt. And if you get caught, it's gonna be bad."

"I know Justin, but I gotta at least try," He pleaded, "I can't just let them win...I'm not going to let them turn me into one of their robots."

"Ok, Daniel," Justin conceded, "but we need to think this out a little better before we try. And if we decide to go, we should all go together. Who knows, we might not get another shot."

Daniel was happier now that they hadn't completely dismissed his idea. He began explained to the rest of the group how the escape would work. Justin, Peter and Carrie listened intently, interjecting their own ideas. They were so focused on what they were doing they didn't notice that the shadows beneath the bedroom door had shifted slightly.

5
CONFORMATION

Justin sat upright in bed, his heart racing. Something had wakened him but his mind, still groggy, couldn't figure out what it was. He looked around the bedroom trying to see where all of the commotion was coming from. The sun had just begun to crest the horizon and streams of light invaded the room. He was able to make out Peter's figure, still in bed clutching the blankets around his chin. He wasn't making any noise. He sat there just as confused as Justin. Daniel didn't know what the commotion was but he knew it wasn't good. In one deft leap he descended from the top bunk and headed for the door. His hand reached for the doorknob but he was too late. The door was thrown open by 639 and two school security officers. Daniel tried to rush past them but they were prepared for something like that. They grabbed Daniel and threw him to the ground before placing wrist restraints on him.

Now that the door was open, Justin could hear where all the screaming was coming from, Jennifer and Carries room. He could make out Carrie's voice and she sounded hysterical. However, he didn't have much time to contemplate the fate of his friend because he was in enough trouble of his own. Leaving Daniel face down on the ground, the officers pulled Peter and Justin out of their beds and into the hallway. They shoved them up against the wall and told them to stand at attention and wait. While Daniel was being hauled off by the security, 639 stayed to question the other two boys.

"Both of you come with me," 639 said glaring at Justin and Peter. They weren't even given time to change into their clothes but were taken downstairs in their pajamas and put into two separate offices. Justin didn't know what had happened to Carrie but assumed her fate was similar to his own. He had seen Matron leading her downstairs; poor Carrie was crying uncontrollably. He didn't see Jennifer at all but was sure she wasn't being pulled into any of this mess.

Justin sat in the leather chair waiting to be questioned, shaking in terror. 639 stood in front of him, arms folded across his chest. Justin had never seen him look so angry. "Do you want to tell me what you and the other children have been up to or am I going to have to force you to tell me."

"No sir," Justin's voice trembled.

"No sir what? No, you aren't going to tell me or no, I'm not going to have to force you?" 639 continued pressing Justin for answers.

"There's nothing to tell sir," Justin continued.

"Really? You have nothing to tell me? How about sneaking out of your room at night?" The more Justin avoided the questions, the louder 639's voice became.

"I don't know what you're talking about sir," Justin continued to play the innocent.

"I know you've been sneaking out of your room. Are you going to sit there and lie to me?" 639 looked at him incredulously. He couldn't believe that this unpleasant child had the audacity to come against him.

Justin sat there, head down and didn't respond.

"How about your plans to escape," 639 pushed.

"We didn't have any plans to escape, "Justin argued half heartedly.

"I'm not stupid boy," 639 continued, "I saw the register, I heard about your plans, I know everything!" Still not getting a response from Justin 639 moved on to the next question. "Who else is involved in this escape?"

Justin refused to budge from his story. "No one, there is no escape planned."

"I'm not wasting any more time with you Justin. I only hope your friend Peter is smarter than you." 639 walked over to the door and opened it beckoning security. Then, turning to Justin he said, "Maybe some time in the box will help you remember."

The color slowly drained from Justin's face and his eyes were the size of saucers, still he remained silent. Justin was taken by the arm and escorted to a small building at the back of the orphanage that once housed a caretaker. It was now where they did their more radical reprogramming; one in particular was referred to as the black box.

He was walked down a dimly lit hall to a steel black door. The guard took out a massive key and put it in the slot. With a loud clank the door was unlocked and pulled open. Justin couldn't bring himself to walk into the "black box", he had to be shoved in from behind. Once the door was closed he couldn't see a thing. From the seconds the door had been open he was able to see a small square room. It was only big enough for a metal chair which sat in the center of the room and a small plastic bucket in the corner to be used as a toilet.

As soon as the light went out, Justin began to panic. It seemed hard to breathe; the air was warm and thick. Justin took several deep breaths to dispel the feeling he was going to suffocate. The odor hanging in the air from the used and un-emptied bucket added to the uncomfortable environment of the room. After several successful breaths, Justin realized there was plenty of air in the room. He began to calm down a little and inched his way over to the chair and sat.

The whole thing seemed surreal to him; like he was still lying in his bed dreaming. Justin was not only scared for himself but for his friends as well. He wondered what was happening to them right now. Well, at least he knew no one was enduring the black box. Peter was probably being interrogated by 639 and Carrie by Matron. What was happening to Daniel though was unclear. It seemed like they believed him to be responsible for everything on their list of offenses. And they were more aggressive with him; Justin feared that his punishment would be more severe as well. How they got their information was a little clearer to Justin; he assumed it was provided by Jennifer. He wasn't really mad at her though, she was just a kid. There wasn't anything she or anyone of them could have done to stop the brainwashing. He wasn't sure what the others would say while being questioned but Justin was determined not to give them any information. He could never live with the fact that he caused his friends to get into trouble. He had already lost one family and wasn't about to risk losing another.

Justin fidgeted on the hard chair for what seemed like an eternity. His stomach was beginning to growl loudly from the missed meal and he needed to use the toilet. However, he wasn't ready to try the makeshift one in the corner. He figured he could hold out for a while longer; hopefully in time to be released. Unfortunately Justin didn't realize that his time there was going to be extended. The orphanage needed to make sure each one of them would never attempt to rebel again. They would accomplish that goal regardless of the cost.

Eventually Justin became tired of sitting and decided to walk around the dark room. He reached his hand out to touch the wall lightly with his fingertips and used them to guide him. The journey wasn't a long one, the room being quite small. After completing several circles around the perimeter, Justin sat back down. He didn't know how long he'd been in there but he was already bored. To pass the time and get his mind off of his full bladder and empty stomach, Justin began reciting every story he could remember his mother reading to him as a child. When those memories were exhausted Justin resorted to reciting his times tables. Finally he couldn't hold out any longer; he headed over to the bucket in the corner and relieved himself. It was so dark that he had no idea where he was aiming but at that point didn't really care as long as it was in the opposite direction from where he was sitting. Afterwards he wiped his hands on his pajama pants disgusted he had nothing to wash them with.

Once back in the chair, Justin did everything he could think of to pass the time; he talked to himself, sang, yelled at his invisible jailers, and eventually cried. He wished his parents had never kept those stupid books. If they hadn't he would have never been forced to go to the orphanage and they would still be alive. He missed them dearly but there was a part of him that was angry at them; angry that they had caused this to happen. They were the parents; they were supposed to look out for him. And look, he was sitting in the middle of the black box being punished, scared and alone. After several more minutes of frustrated tears Justin sighed deeply. Of course he couldn't blame them; they would never have wanted this to happen to him. Emotionally empty and resigned to the fact that he might be there awhile, Justin felt extremely tired.

He got up and pushed the chair out of the way with his foot. Slowly crouching down, he felt around the floor to make sure it was clear for him to lie down. There wasn't enough room for him to spread out so he pulled himself into a tight ball and tried to imagine he was in his own bed at home. Eventually he did fall asleep but was plagued by violent nightmares.

Several hours later he was awakened by the sound of footsteps in the hallway. His heart raced with fear as the footsteps came closer and then stopped outside the door. Then, the door opened abruptly and a tray was slid across the floor. Before Justin's eyes could even adjust to the light, the door was slammed shut again. He stretched his hands outward across the floor feeling around for the tray. He was past the point of being hungry, he was starved! His fingers immediately identified the crust of a piece of bread. There was another item on the tray that Justin picked up and smelled before trying; it was a piece of hard cheese. He took small bites trying to avoid the occasional bitter taste of mold. When he wasn't successful, Justin quickly spit it out onto the metal food tray. He washed everything down with the cup of water that was provided. After his meager meal Justin felt oddly relaxed and removed from the situation. He often found himself having this queer sensation after eating or drinking anything at the orphanage and it scared him. This time, however, he was thankful for the peace it brought. He fell asleep again and didn't wake until his next meal was brought to him. He wasn't sure how many days he was there; it seemed like one very long night. When they finally opened the door to release him from his temporary prison, he was so weak he had to be carried to his room. Of course this room wasn't the same he had shared with the boys; he was given a new one in general population. Peter was also reassigned a room on the other end of the building, far from his friend. He weren't sure where Carrie was housed now but it was far from their original room. And none of them had seen what happened to Daniel; in fact, the morning that they were dragged from their rooms was the last time any of them ever saw him.

They no longer had the freedom to speak during meals or to and from classes; they were given an escort everywhere. Even though security was stepped up, it wasn't really necessary. Since their ordeal they were all a little more pliable. The daily medication administered by Doctor X also helped them realize the error of their ways and great reformation with open arms.

If asked, Justin couldn't pinpoint one specific moment in time when he became enlightened and embraced the truth of the government. It was a natural progression for them all; the old had passed away and the new and improved had taken hold.

6
THE REAL WORLD

On the day of his eighteenth birthday, Justin was unceremoniously escorted to the door of the orphanage and released. It was almost like he had gained early release from a life sentence in prison. Spending so much time behind bars had made the world a strange and unfamiliar place. Like most people leaving the orphanage, he didn't have any family to help with the transition. And, there was nothing left of the friendships that he had on the inside. That was all gone thanks to the guidance of Greenville staff. There were many times as a young boy in the orphanage that Justin longed for his freedom. Now with that freedom in his grasp, he wasn't really sure what to do with it.

Fortunately, the young adults leaving the orphanage weren't completely on their own, the government gave them temporary assistance. They were given a spending card with several thousand international credits for food, clothing and other necessities. They were also given a place to live and a new working assignment. The apartment complex was only a few blocks from the orphanage and every one of the eighty units was occupied by a new release. The lease on the apartment was good for one year, after that Justin was expected to find his own place. The same was true for the job. If he did a good job there was a chance that he would retain the position. If not, it would be up to him to find something else and quickly. The government was always happy to help but it had its limits. There wasn't room for laziness or unproductively in this new and improved society. Everyone had a part to play and if they weren't willing to participate, they would be replaced with someone who was. Fortunately, Justin showed a real knack for the technology sector which made him very employable and gave him special privileges. Everything they depended on revolved around some sort of technology. And, if it didn't exist, Justin was the man to make it happen.   Every employer he worked with throughout his career was thrilled at his natural talent to form something out of nothing, especially the government.   They needed new talent to replace all those who'd crossed the doors of judgment and lost their lives.   Justin was perfect, he was young, he was talented, and he was completely rehabilitated by the orphanage. In fact, they considered him to be one of their greatest success stories.

If they could have looked at the real Justin and seen what was going on inside, they wouldn't have been so proud of their efforts. Justin was a master at hiding his true feelings. He never felt like he quite fit in. He would look at the other students in the orphanage, their wholehearted acceptance and love for the new order and he just didn't get it. There was always something that nagged him deep down inside. Those unsettling thoughts and feelings followed him into adulthood. He wasn't one of them and he knew it. Unfortunately, what troubled him the most was he didn't know who he really was. Every morning before he left the house he would have to mentally prepare himself. He was afraid someone would see something in him that was considered dangerous to society. Everyone he encountered daily, his co-workers, the people he passed on the streets, they went through the motions of life without complaining with a compliant smile echoing the emptiness inside. For Justin, it took everything he had not to rebel. There was one thing the orphanage had been successful at; they had taught him to fear the government and its punishments. That was the only thing that kept him in line.

Justin was quickly picked up by the temporary employer, World Tech Corporation, when they saw how talented he was. They got their money from government contracts; the more Justin could produce, the more valuable he was. Justin was all too eager to comply; his job was one thing he actually enjoyed doing. It kept him busy and he often spent long nights and weekends at the lab. This also gave him favor with his boss as well as the government. In three years Justin shot up through the company and landed the position of Director of Scientific Technologies. He was only twenty-one but he had power and lots of money to go along with it. His new position and the six figure salary also brought unwanted attention from the president of World Tech Corporation's secretary, Dawn Casanas. She began approaching Justin on a regular basis trying to convince him to go out with her. Justin declined every time but Dawn wasn't one to take no for an answer. One morning several months after starting in his new role as director she approached him again. Justin was walking down the office hallway engrossed in reading the case study reports on a recent technology when she came out of nowhere and blocked his progression.

"Hi Justin," Dawn exclaimed in mock surprise, "I didn't even see you coming down the hall! How are you?"

"In a hurry," he replied without looking up from his electronic tablet.

"Of course," she giggled, "I wouldn't want to keep you from your work."

"Then don't" he replied looking directly into her eyes. He began to move past her when she shifted her position to stop him directly in his tracks.

Justin, beginning to get annoyed, stated, "What do you want Dawn? I really need to get back to work."

"I know, I was just wondering if you wanted to go out tonight for a drink. A friend of mine just opened a great little wine tasting bar and I really want to try it out," she said quickly before he could get away from her.

"I don't drink" Justin retorted.

"Well, how about we just go get a cup of coffee, that way we can have a chance to talk," she pressed.

"I don't have the time. I have a lot of work to do," he responded shortly.

"That's what you always say," Dawn pouted.

"Look," Justin continued in a more friendly tone, "I appreciate the offer but I keep my professional relationships completely professional."

"Are you sure there isn't anything I can do to change your mind?" she asked seductively, pouting her lips and batting her overly made up eyes at him.

He stifled back a laugh before responding curtly, "Sorry, no," and turned before she could say another word. He walked directly to his office, closed the door and locked. She was relentless! When he first joined the firm he tried to be cordial, wishing her a "good morning" or saying a "how are you" as they passed in the hall. He learned his lesson quickly. Encouraged by the fact he spoke to her, she would follow him around everywhere and flirt every chance she got. Once, when she wasn't quite paying attention, she followed him into the men's room. Fortunately there wasn't anyone else in there using the facilities. Once she saw the urinals lined up against the wall she realized her mistake and left the room, embarrassed but not ready to give up. Giving her the cold shoulder was what Justin was reduced to; it didn't stop her it just slowed her down. Fortunately he wasn't the only male in the office and once she struck out with Justin that day, she moved on to another victim.

For the next four years it was more of the same; Justin lived and breathed his work. When he was headfirst in some new technology he didn't notice how miserable he was.

Justin was true to his word when he told Dawn that day that he didn't drink. However, some frustrated and unhappy years later all of that changed. It was shortly after his twenty-fifth birthday when Justin took his first drink. It wasn't something he ever thought about doing before and if it hadn't been offered, he might have gone through life without the knowledge of alcohol and its affects. But, once he tried it, he was hooked. It was actually at a work function that he was introduced to what would become his first love. It even surpassed the love he had for his job. He had just been given a big promotion at the company for one of his inventions. The technology brought incredible improvements to what was being used now for corrector surveillance equipment. The government was able to procure more evidence, easier and faster and in turn bring more people to judgment. And, it was all due to Justin's work. He was a superstar in his field and made outstanding contributions to the new order.

That day at work he smiled appropriately while his co-workers congratulated him on completing another successful project. He shook the hand of his boss, Mr. Jensen, and listened to him drone on for an hour about how excited the government was at the new technology and how much money it was going to make them. He even managed to hold back his disgust as his coworker, Dawn Casanas', flirted mercilessly with everyone in the office. He did everything he was supposed to do and when he was handed a drink, he drank it down. And then he followed it with another, and then another.

This became a normal routine for Justin. Every day he went to work, played the wonder boy for ten or twelve hours, and then came home to the bottle. Of course he was careful not to overdo it. Just like disease, addiction of any kind was unacceptable. If it appeared that Justin had a drinking problem he would immediately be put on a watch list. He was very careful only to drink at home and to hide its effects when around others. The years he spent on the farm he learned a lot about herbs and natural remedies for just about anything. Peppermint for the stomach, willow bark for the headache, fennel, century leaf, and a few other ingredients steeped into a tea became part of Justin's morning routine.

He had no secrets to keep outside of work. Justin was very private and made no attempts to get close to anyone. He had no friends and had never met anyone who he would be remotely interested in dating. The bottle was the only thing that understood him and it was the only place he found comfort and enough peace to finally fall asleep at night.

One Friday several months after the office party, Justin was more unsettled than most days. He had a continual nagging feeling he was forgetting something, something very important. The more he tried to remember, the more it seemed to evade him. Always there but never there, it was maddening! That was what drove him to the bottle; it was what made him feel so hopeless. Justin figured if he couldn't remember then he would do whatever he could to forget.

As soon as he arrived home that day he hurried into the house, anxious for some relief. He slammed the front door behind him, took off his jacket, and went straight for the liquor cabinet in the dining buffet. After grabbing a bottle of vodka and a glass, he plopped down into the nearest stuffed chair. He opened the bottle and inhaled deeply. To Justin, the fragrance was as sweet as any flower. He poured himself a healthy amount in the glass and eagerly put it up to his lips. The alcohol ran over his tongue and down his throat spreading warmth throughout his body. He drank one smooth glass after the other until the bottle was empty. He stared at the bottle for a few dazed seconds before holding it up and tipping it over. He watched as the last couple of drops ran slowly down the neck of the bottle. It hung on for an eternity before dropping into the glass waiting below. "Not even enough to make me forget my life". He turned to look at the time flashing on the holographic media panel on the wall. It was only 8:00 pm. "Great..." Justin sighed, running his hand through his thick brown hair. He thought about getting up and getting another bottle but that's as far as it went. He passed out right where he sat. The sound of the glass shattering as it slipped through his fingers and hit the floor wasn't enough to wake him. Justin drank enough to make him pass out and forget about how miserable he was. Unfortunately his dreams weren't able to bring him any peace either.

When Justin awoke the next morning his first conscious thought, which was his last subconscious thought the night before, flashed through his head. It was a memory of the flames engulfing his family's home as he sat in the corrector's cruiser waiting to be taken to the orphanage. He sat up in bed and remained there stunned at first and then began to cry softly. The tears weren't only for the family he had lost; they were for the joy in remembering. It was the first clear memory he had since he was in the orphanage.

Those images played through Justin's mind the rest of the day. Although the memories were of a traumatic time, they sparked something new inside of him. It was a little twinge right where his heart was which made him feel something entirely foreign. Justin didn't know what it meant but it made him feel alive.

7
RECOVERING WHAT'S LOST

Justin chugged down his magic hangover remedy while slipping on his blue dress shirt. Hangovers were bad enough but when you mixed it with a Monday morning it was doubly depressing. Worse still, he had a meeting first thing with his boss. Phillip Jensen was a tough supervisor who was always pushing Justin for more. The first Monday of every month Justin was summoned to his office and had to give an accounting of everything he was working on. He also had to be prepared to debate the pros and cons of any whim of an idea Mr. Jensen threw at him.

"Good morning Justin, this should only take a few minutes. I've already read the reports you sent me last week on the *i*vision Eye-Cam. I'm pretty happy with what you have so far. Is there anything you want to add?" Mr. Jensen questioned.

"No sir, I've included the schematics of the implant with the report. The rest is pretty straightforward. Everything picked up by the eye-cam will immediately be uploaded to the Global Life History database. Besides the incredible visuals, there is audio capture up to 100 meters." Justin reported confidently. He was very proud of his achievements with this technology.

Mr. Jensen didn't seem as impressed and voiced his concerns, "100 meters isn't far Justin. Can't we do better than that?"

"Of course sir, the 100 meter video capture comes with the standard model. We can adjust the audio for surveillance up to 3,000 meters. We can also match the video with the audio." Justin added.

"Wonderful! What about the rejection rate?" Jensen asked.

Justin referred to his notes as he responded to Jensen's answers, "Zero in our test subjects. We won't have real world test results until they are on the market for at least a year. The projections are good though."

"Have you added the bonus feature we talked about?" Jensen asked pointedly.

This was one thing Justin wasn't proud of. However, it wasn't like he could go against the government's request. He answered the question reluctantly. "Yes, the kill switch was added per the government's request, though I don't see why that was necessary."

"Who are we to question the government? After all, they pay us very well for the work we do. I don't care what they ask for Walker, we deliver without question." Phillip said slowly and deliberately.

"Of course sir, you are completely right. I'm sure they have reasons for everything they do, even if someone like me doesn't understand them." Justin hurriedly covered.

"That's right Justin," Mr. Jensen continued, "its best if we don't forget our place in the big scheme of things."

Justin shook his head in agreement, glad the conversation was over.

"Ok, now that we've got that settled, could you do me a favor and hand this to Ms. Casanas on the way out?"

"Sure, "Justin replied, taking the paper from Jensen's outstretched hand. As he turned to leave he glanced down at the memo and stopped, his eyebrows furrowed in puzzlement as he read.

"The Government Advisory Board will be visiting our offices next Friday, at 0600 hours. They want to find out if there is any *truth* behind the claims that the *l*vision Eye-Cam *will* be more cost effective and reliable than what they are currently using. Their determination will be invaluable when we *set* the retail price. I want *you* to send them ten units to try for *free* prior to their visit. "

P. Jensen

The truth will set you free; these words jumped out at him from the page. "What's this supposed to mean?" The words were out of Justin's mouth before he had time to think.

"What? What are you talking about Walker? I told you it's a memo for Ms. Casanas," he answered a bit curtly. When he was finished with a conversation, he was finished.

"No, I mean the words that are sticking out, what is it supposed to mean," pushed Justin.

"I don't know what you're talking about. It is a straightforward memo," Phillip stood up and started to walk towards Justin.

"The truth will set you free," Justin muttered under his breath. Phillip grabbed the paper out of his hand and looked it over. "What are you talking about? I don't see anything unusual about this memo Walker. Are you all right? You look a little pale?"

Justin quickly regained his composure and put up his hand to stop Mr. Phillip from paging the company medic. "Of course sir, I'm all right, just a little tired," he explained quickly in an attempt to reassure him, "I guess it's just the lighting, the lettering looked weird. I'll give it to her on my way out." He quickly left before Mr. Phillip could continue.

Justin went back to his office and locked the door behind him. He sat at his desk trying to figure out what was going on. Those words he saw on the paper, he knew them. He had seen that passage somewhere before. Like everything else he just couldn't remember how he knew it. Obviously it was from his past, which made it something dangerous. If he slipped up and someone thought he was remembering too much, he might be sent in for a little additional reprogramming. Unable to jog his memory, Justin pushed it aside and went back to work. He continued working late into the night and made it home just in time to get a few hours of sleep.

That night Justin had another dream but this time it was about his father. They were sitting next to the fireplace in the living room reading the Bible. His father was reading scripture to him and Justin found the words and the sound of his voice very comforting. It seemed like the dream went on for hours and hours; just him and his dad. He wished he could have stayed in that place of warmth and peace forever. He was a little disappointed when his alarm announced the new day and he was forced to wake up. However, that feeling and the last thing his father read to him, John 8:32 "And you will know the truth and the truth shall set you free" stayed with him the rest of the day.

Justin was really confused. Between the memo yesterday and the dream last night; someone was trying to tell him something. He was also really excited because now he was sure his memory was coming back. He just wished it would happen a little faster. However, bits and pieces was far better than none at all. He sat behind the wheel of his car on the way to work in Lower Darby, not paying attention to the road. His mind was too preoccupied with everything going on. His life seemed to have taken a weird turn somewhere and he wasn't sure where it was going to end up. Without realizing it, Justin ended up on the old dirt road which led to the ashes of the once beloved home. Justin slowly pulled down the long cobblestone drive, "What am I doing?" he thought as he quickly looked in the rearview mirror to make sure he wasn't followed. Although thoughts of insanity crossed his mind, he continued up the drive and pulled to a stop where the front door used to be. He sat there several minutes before getting out of the car. He rested his shaking hands on the steering wheel trying to steady them. When he felt a little calmer, Justin opened the door and got out. The first thing he did was walk around the remains of the foundation. Most of the bricks were still intact and several charred timbers were lying haphazardly across it. The burnt house was a grim memorial to the family that once lived there. The garden his mother loved so dearly was overgrown with brambles. Broken pieces of the small white picket fence which once stood as its boundary, now stuck up through the thicket. Speckles of color could still be seen between the growth as wildflowers tried desperately to push through and reach the sun's rays.   A sharp pain stuck at his heart as he looked around at the overgrown fields he used to play in.   All these memories washed over him as he stared motionless and reveled in remembrance. "Wow," Justin exclaimed stunned. It was incredible! Laughing for the first time in years he thought, "I guess the orphanage wasn't as good as they thought they were."

He almost hated to leave but he was supposed to be at work a half hour ago and he was never late. "Better get back before I'm missed," he said aloud and climbed back behind the wheel. "Work," Justin voiced the command and let the car do the driving.   As he got closer to his destination he realized his foolishness. He shouldn't have gone out there today in broad daylight, what if he had been seen?

When Justin walked into the building and looked up at the time display on the wall panel, he saw that he was actually an hour late. Of course it didn't go unnoticed. As he walked past Dawn's desk on the way to his office, he could see her disapproving frown. Justin didn't care, he didn't report to her. He was an important man to the government so he could come and go freely. It just wasn't like him to be late for work; even if just for a few minutes.

Justin walked into his office and closed the door tightly behind him. He rolled up his sleeves and went into the adjoining restroom to splash a little water on his face. "Get a grip," he told his reflection sternly. He couldn't go around acting like something was wrong or he might have his own inventions used on him. He took a few deep breaths and walked back out to his office and started going through the mound of paperwork that was strewn across his desk. He created masterpieces of technology but he hated the paperwork that went along with it. It would be another long night at the office but maybe it would keep his mind off of everything else.

That night when Justin got home from work he was exhausted. He made himself a little dinner, leftover chicken from the day before and a salad, changed his clothes, and went directly to bed. It was the first time he fell into bed without having a drink or two first. It wasn't like he made a conscious decision not to drink; it never even crossed his mind. He was sound asleep minutes after his head touched the pillow.

His dreams centered on his father for the second night in a row. Justin was in the kitchen sitting at the table eating a peanut butter and jelly sandwich. His dad was telling him about the fish he had just caught down at the creek. As his father's story went on, the fish got bigger. Justin laughed in his sleep thoroughly enjoying the dream. Unfortunately, before his dad was finished with the story, the front door was broken down and correctors began invading the home. His father hurried to his side, crouched down until he was eye level with Justin and grabbed the front of his shirt and shouted, " "Hurry Justin, Hurry!"

Justin woke up in a panic his heart thudding loudly in his chest. The dream felt so real it took him several minutes to calm down. He eventually lay back down and tried to go to sleep. Unfortunately that wasn't going to happen. "Damn" Justin groaned as he jumped out of bed and began to get dressed in a pair of dark pants and sweater. It was in the middle of the night but he felt compelled to go back to the family home. "This is just nuts," he muttered to himself as he grabbed a light stick and headed out to the car. He traced his route back to the house and sat in the driveway for about twenty minutes, headlights dimmed, before gathering enough courage to get out.

Once he left the safe confines of the vehicle he made his way over to the remains of the stone foundation. Fortunately, it was still partially intact. Justin's heart began to race and sweat dripped from his brow even though the night air was cool. "Could it really be there?" he thought as his fingertips rubbed against the cool stonework. He could feel the unevenness of the stone and then, there it was, a small dip in the mortar. Justin's hands were a bit bigger now and his finger didn't quite fit into the small hole but that wasn't going to stop him. He made several attempts to pry out the brick but only managed to scrape a few layers off of his finger. It was no use; he had to do something else. He paused and stared at the stone a few minutes deep in thought. Justin figured there had to be something in the car that he could use. He ran back to the car and began rummaging through the interior. What he found was the gold pen that was given to him in recognition of his outstanding work. At least he found a good use for it. Justin took it back to the brick and poked the tip into the slot and began working it back and forth. "If they saw what I was using this for I'd be judged in an instant," Justin muttered. Eventually the stone loosened enough for Justin to pull it out. Justin's secret hiding place was finally opened. There lie Justin's treasures. He moved aside the baseball cards and army men to get to his most prized possession. It was a small book with the words "Holy Bible" inlayed in gold print on the cover. Inside was an inscription from his mother. "Justin, in this book you will find everything you need to truly live. Keep it close to your heart. Love, mom."

The pages were weathered and yellowed from spending all those years hidden in the basement. But, the book was still in great condition. He began to leaf through the pages when off in the distance he heard the snap of a breaking branch. Startled, he stuffed the book in the waist of his pants and pulled his shirt over the top to hide the leather bound book from site. He then quickly headed back to the car. The other items lay there where he found them, forgotten pieces of his past. No need for them anymore, he'd gotten what he came for.

8
FINDING TRUTH

Before his eyes were even open, Justin slipped his hand under the pillow to make sure the book was still there. Not that it could have gone anywhere but somehow checking made him feel better. Last night when he finally arrived home he was feeling a little paranoid. He must have looked out of the windows ten times before realizing no one had followed him there.

However, the next morning he felt much better. A good night's sleep had cleared his thoughts and put his anxiousness at bay. Justin showered, dressed and then sat down at the kitchen counter with a cup of hot coffee. The Bible lay on the surface in front of him, unopened since he found it the night before. He sat there holding the coffee cup in one hand while the other tapped the top of the Bible.

"Now, what?" Justin thought. He knew the price he would have to pay if anyone found out he had a Bible in his possession. His parents had paid with their lives, he wouldn't be any different. "Just doesn't make much sense." Justin said aloud. He picked up the Bible and looked at it intently, "Why would they be afraid of one little book?" He spent hours reading the Bible with his family, somewhere deep down inside was the answer to all this craziness. He had to know what it was and he believed the key to remembering was in his hand.

Before leaving for work, Justin buried the Bible under a stack of dirty laundry. Not the best hiding place but good enough for now. He wasn't under any suspicion so there was little chance anyone would be searching his house. However, the effort made him feel his little secret would remain secure. When he arrived home after work, the Bible was waiting for him right where he left it.

Justin finished his dinner, got ready for bed, and then pulled the Bible from its hiding place. He got into bed and opened the cover of the book. "Where should I begin?" he thought, "I guess the best place would be at the beginning." He opened his Bible to Genesis "In the beginning God created the heavens and the earth...." Justin softly repeated the words on each of the pages to let their message soak in. He continued reading far into the night, putting it away only when his fatigued eyes caused his vision to blur.

As he went through the next day, Justin thought about everything he'd read. It was so different from the teachings at the orphanage and the general beliefs of the new order. Its message offered a freedom that would be very dangerous if shared, no wonder the government had destroyed all that they found. Justin wondered if there was anyone else out there that knew the truth. Maybe one day he would be able to find out.

The next several months Justin continued to read the word of God. He even brought the Bible to work with him but was very careful to avoid being caught with it. It would be a shame to have come so far and learned so much only to have it taken from him and added to the government's burn pile.

Justin had a lot of unanswered questions as his analytical brain tried to make sense of the scripture. He was also hung up on the fact that, if there was a God, why had all these terrible things happened to him. He knew that there was something that he was missing; he wasn't sure what, but he continued to read hoping to find out.

His daily diet of the Word of God was making a huge difference in the way Justin saw the world. In fact, you could say he was finally able to see if for what it was. He had clarity and a peace that was foreign to this new generation. His time in the scriptures was something of great value. He knew that change would have to come because he could no longer function as the "old" Justin. He could no longer ignore the injustice and oppression of the government and he could no longer partake and contribute to its bounty. Change was coming and he wanted to make sure he was prepared for when that day arrived.

A week later as he was leaving the office, Dawn

Casanas stopped him at the door. "Mr. Jensen needs you to sign off on this notice before you leave. It just says we will be crediting you the bonus as of Friday morning. Justin sighed heavily, in a hurry to get home. "Ok, just a sec," he replied and began digging though his portfolio looking for a pen. Feeling around in the bottom of the leather satchel his fingers came in contact with a pen and he quickly pulled it out. "Here we go," he said holding it up.

"What happened to that? It looks like an animal chewed on it?" Dawn asked as she peered intently at the mangled pen.

Not responding, Justin grabbed the paper out of her hand, signed it, and handed it back to her. He stuffed the gold pen back into the bag and then gathered everything up again to leave "Was there anything else?" He asked impatiently.

"Ahh, I guess not," she said slowly. However, she remained glued to the spot and stared at him as intently as she had at the pen.

"Yes?" he asked with annoyance.

"Well, you look different," Dawn said slowly as if trying to figure out what had changed.

"What are you talking about?" Justin asked irritated that she continued to hold him up.

"I don't know, just different." She said, eyebrows drawn as if inspecting him in detail.

Justin was starting to feel uncomfortable and he

didn't want to waste any more time talking to Dawn. He said the first thing he could think of, "Are you hitting on me?" he asked in mock admonishment, trying to end the uncomfortable exchange.

"Ah..of course not Mr. Walker. I'm sorry; I need to get back to work." She quickly turned and began to walk away. Of course it wasn't fast enough for her to hide the fact that her face had turned a bright red.

"Have a nice day Ms. Casanas" Justin threw the comment over his shoulder as he exited the building. He breathed a sigh of relief; he was finally on the road home. Remembering her words, Justin's first stop when he entered his house was the nearest mirror. He looked closely at the face staring back at him trying to see what she was talking about. There was something different about the way he looked. His brown eyes seemed brighter, his face was a healthier color and the circles under his eyes seemed less noticeable now that he was sleeping without the aid of alcohol.

"Wow, I guess I do look different," Justin said somewhat surprised he hadn't noticed it before. His guess was that the change was so gradual it was easy for him to overlook. Besides, he usually only looked in the mirror in the morning while getting ready for the day. And half the time he wasn't quite awake. Now that it was pointed out, it was pretty obvious. Justin was thirty-three years old and he looked better now than he did ten years ago.

Justin had been keeping his eyes open looking for that opportunity to make a "change". He was surprised when a month later change came looking for him. He just left the lab to go to lunch when two gentlemen approached him from either side. At first Justin panicked thinking they were controllers. He calmed down when he realized they were actually recruiters from GlobalIWitness. They had been waiting for an opportunity away from work in which to approach him. Apparently, they were interested in hiring him to fill a government contract. He didn't like their tactics and their reputation wasn't very good either. The company had close ties to the government and was nothing to mess around with; they could completely destroy your career or your life. Promising he would consider the offer, Justin informed them that he would need some time to make a decision. Besides, they could wait, they needed him much more than he needed them.

After putting off the call for a couple of days, Justin decided to take the position. Ordinarily he wouldn't have considered their offer but they had something that he wanted, information. GlobalIWitness was responsible for retrieving and storing all of the data that was filtered through the eye-cams. They had been the government's choice for over thirty years. He had a lot of unanswered questions about his parents, grandfather, and his dear friends at the orphanage that needed answered. This job was the one way he could finally get some closure. Justin gave notice at World Tech Corporation and two weeks later started at GlobalWitness.

The first day of work was a little unnerving for Justin. Normally it wouldn't faze him to start a new position. He was talented and was able to meet or exceed each of his employer's expectations without effort. No, this job was different. He was standing at a door that had been locked for many years. It was now wide open, ready for him to walk through.

By the time he finally got to the building and entered, he was filled with an anxious excitement. Justin felt more alive that day then he ever had before. The director, Thomas Mannan, walked towards him, hand extended. He grasped Justin's hand firmly and shook it while welcoming him. "This is it Mr. Walker, you've made it to the top. You should be proud of yourself, not many people have walked through this building or seen what you're about to see."

"I'm extremely honored to be here sir, "Justin responded enthusiastically. The tour Mannan gave him included the lab Justin would be sharing, the cafeteria, infirmary, his office, and lastly, the recording room. Mannan swiped the back of his hand across the sensor in the upper corner of the door and it magically opened. Seeing Justin's confusion, he explained, "Implant, in a few years everyone will have one. Right now they are a little big and have to be surgically implanted. We need them to be small enough to inject under the skin of the hand. That's one of the things you will be in charge of while you're here."

"What's the purpose of an implant? Wouldn't a thumb print or retina scan work just as well?" questioned Justin.

"It doesn't just open doors Justin. You're a pioneer in the field of technology surely you can come up with something better than that." He paused for a few seconds and waited for a response. Not getting one, he continued, "No? Come on, use your imagination. This chip contains everything I am, my likes, dislikes, financial records, where and what I ate last night, and how many times I brush my teeth a day, "

"Why do you really need to save information like that?"Justin continued, not impressed.

"Freedom, absolute freedom! I never have to worry about money or appointments or anything. Eventually I'll be able to swipe it at the grocery store and it will order everything for me and then have it delivered right to my house. Or go to my favorite restaurant and swipe it and voila! Here comes my dinner, just how I like it and already paid for." Mannan continued proudly.

Carefully Justin pushed with his questions, "Who has access to all this information?"

"Well, no one….except the government of course," Mannan volunteered.

"Why would they care where you eat or how many times you brush your teeth?" Justin was appalled at what he was hearing. The displeasure he felt slipped out of his mouth before he had time to think about it.

"Now Justin, don't be sarcastic. Let's say you haven't been doing your exercise or you've been eating poorly. Well of course the government has a right to know. Then, they can step in and make sure you are taken care of. Since they are responsible for your health insurance, they should be responsible for your health. Ultimately the government is best qualified to make decisions for the people." His boss explained patiently.

Justin couldn't believe how eagerly people accepted the government and their control over their lives. "Doesn't that just turn us into robots, not even thinking for ourselves?"

Mannan, not deterred by Justin's attitude, went on to enlighten him. "Look at the history of man, Justin. When left on our own, we have destroyed ourselves with over indulgence, lust and greed. We've stripped the planet of its natural resources and polluted the air and water. Man needs to have someone to guide them, make choices for them, and provide them with what they need. Gustov Baccus has literally become the savior of this world. If it wasn't for him and the government he helped set up, I hate to think where we'd all be right now."

Justin stood there unable to think of anything acceptable to say. He just nodded his head as though he finally "got it". His position there was too important to mess up on the first day of work. Smiling Justin looked to the open door, "I can't wait to see what's inside."

"Yes this is our pride and joy." Mannan boasted like a proud parent. They walked into the massive room "This is where all the magic happens. We receive all the data from thousands of correctors, sort it, and send the pertinent information along to the government. Of course a copy of everything is uploaded to the mega-computer, the Global Life History database."

"Incredible," Justin said taking in the massive computers lining the walls. Several dozen large computer monitors hung on the opposite flashing images so quickly it was difficult to actually see what was happening. There was also a control station in the center of the room with two separate computers used for retrieving information. Inside this room was everything he needed.

"Yes, it is isn't it? It's also highly confidential as you can imagine. Not many people have access to this room." Mannan boasted. He really wasn't supposed to bring people in here but he couldn't help himself. The government would have a fit if they found out.

"Of course, that makes sense," Justin agreed with Mannan, "I'm sure security is pretty tight though."

"You would think so but no, it doesn't have to be." Mannan explained.

"What do you mean," questioned Justin.

"Well no one enters this room without this," Mannan said holding up his hand with the implanted chip, "and I've got the only one."

9
ALL IS REVEALED

Now that Justin had been given a job right in the heart of the world's communication center, he was in a perfect position get what he wanted. Accessing the information was easy enough; he could break any code if he had the opportunity. It was getting the opportunity that was the problem. And, once he got the information he wanted, he would need to get out as quickly as possible and disappear. As soon as they found out what he'd done they'd send the controllers out after him.

Justin's first priority was where to go when all of this was over. Yeah, he needed to figure out all of the details of how he was going to get into the room but that could wait. No sense in dwelling on that enormous headache until the first problem was figured out.

He didn't mind so much giving up his home or job and he didn't have anyone special in his life he would miss. By the grace of God, he would be able to live quite comfortably undetected in the woods surrounding his old home. But this would take some planning.

His dad had taught him wilderness survival; what plants and berries were safe to eat, how to start a fire, and how to find fresh water. However, if he planned right, those skills would only be needed in case of emergency. Justin intended to build a makeshift shelter and stock it with dried and canned goods, water, and other necessities. That Saturday morning far before daybreak, Justin loaded his car with what supplies he had laying around the house and headed out. He knew the area well and there were plenty of places in which he could hide.

He arrived at the farm just as the sun began to crest the horizon. Justin pulled in around the back of the remains of the foundation to make his presence less noticeable. No one was going to be out driving in the area but flying surveillance drones made periodic checks on the less populated or abandoned areas around the state. If they noticed anything suspicious, they sent the video to local law enforcement to follow up on. Justin didn't want to wind up on one of their watch lists, especially in the position he was in. Because of his job and the involvement with government contracts, Justin's punishment would be much more severe than most. They couldn't take the chance that one of their own would get out of line.

After making sure the car was hidden, Justin began walking towards the heart of the forest surrounding his farm. He left everything except a hydration bottle and light stick at the car; not wanting to lug it around with him. If he found a spot, he would come back and get the supplies.

But, for now, they remained in his trunk. He attached the hydration bottle to a cord at his waist and then began walking deep into the woods. It was probably further than he had ever gone, even as a young boy.

It was around noon when he finally stopped to take a break. The sun was high overhead but the canopy of trees kept him cool. He sat under a tree and put the hydration bottle up to his lips and took a couple of large swallows. When it was completely emptied, he pressed the small digital display at the bottom to initiate water extraction. The bottle was a great invention, not one of his however, that could remove the moisture right out of the air and purify it for drinking. The first hydration bottle weighed several pounds but, as technology improved, it was scaled back to a few ounces. Justin sat there several more minutes until the bottle was full and then reattached it to the strap at his side. He got up, dusted off his pants, and continued onward.

About an hour later Justin heard the sound of rushing water. He followed the noise until he reached a large creek. Bending down, Justin scooped a handful of the clear fluid and drank it down. Delicious! There was nothing like fresh water right out of a creek. He continued following the winding bank until something caught his eye. Off to the left, deep in the overgrown forest, was a big mass of something. It was hard to tell what exactly; it just looked like a green blob from where he stood. Justin hurried towards it to satiate his curiosity. It turned out to be a large cropping of rocks. They were covered with a thick dense moss which made them hard to identify from a distance. After Justin explored a bit, he found a man sized cave entrance on the side facing a thicket of large oak trees. He grabbed the light stick from his back pants pocket and shined it towards the dark opening. He wanted to make sure he wasn't going to disturb an angry animal before venturing inside. It was perfect! There was more than enough room for a small cot and other supplies. Light shone down from an opening towards the back of the stone ceiling; just enough to permit smoke to escape from a fire pit without being too noticeable. The floor was covered with dirt and some stray plants; nothing too difficult to clear. And to top it off, it wasn't far from a water supply. Justin hurriedly retraced his steps back to the car and began trekking everything he brought to his new home. He stacked the items towards the back wall; a sleeping bag, some canned goods, light sticks, and medical supplies. When he finished, he found some fallen branches and covered his loot. It was highly unlikely anyone would stumble across it out there but it was better not to take any chances. Finished, Justin made it back to the car, exhausted and happy.

Justin spent every Saturday for two months gathering equipment, cleaning out his shelter, and planning for an extended stay. He even managed to hide supplies in strategic areas leading from the city to his cave. When he was ready to run he wouldn't have to worry about running out of supplies. They would be waiting for him. Besides, there might not be time to grab anything extra and the added weight could slow him down.

Justin was finally ready for the next phase of his plan. This one was a little harder than the first and he wasn't quite sure where to start. After a couple of weeks with no progress he was completely frustrated and discouraged.

Justin stood in the shower and let the hot water run over his head and face. "Nothing is ever easy", he thought sighing heavily. He had racked his brain for two weeks without coming up with one feasible idea. He can't get into the recording room without the chip. He can't get the chip unless he convinces Mannan to let him have access to the room. Either that or remove the chip from Mannan's hand and get in himself. Both scenarios were bad ones. There was no way he was going to sweet talk Mannan into letting him peruse the database; that only left surgery on Mannan's hand. Of course, he wasn't going to be a willing participant, and Justin wasn't what you would call a "skilled surgeon".

The only time outside of the kitchen he had used a knife was to gut a deer. Digging the chip out without cutting through an artery would require a little more finesse than cutting through the thick hide of a deer. This was going to present some problems for both he and Mannan.

There were other obstacles as well; Mannan wasn't going to just sit there and let him "have at it". He needed a way to either restrain him or knock him out. Then there was the problem of getting any type of knife past the security desk at work. They scanned everyone entering the building and anything metal would show up on the scanners.

"Ahhh," Justin said aloud getting more frustrated as he thought about it. The problem was that he was in too far; he couldn't go back to the life he was blindly living before. He would prefer death to that. However, he needed to take a mental break from it all and hope for an epiphany. In the mean time, he would go to work and through the motions of being a great employee, dedicated to the company. He also needed to learn Mannan's schedule and find out when and where he could get him alone. That small task was enough for now and Justin felt like it was a good place to start.

Several days later, after thinking through every conceivable idea short of dropping from a helicopter, scaling down the side of the building into Mannan's office, and beating him unconscious, Justin came to the realization it needed to be simple. He needed to rely on what he already knew which was herbs and plants. He knew what to take if you had a hangover, what helped with a headache or upset stomach, and he knew what to do when sleep was hard to come by. Justin also knew of some plants, when combined with alcohol, would make a powerful sleeping compound. In fact, once ingested it would put Mannan to sleep in a matter of minutes or even seconds. He had never actually tried the mixture but his neighbor had broken his leg pretty bad one year and needed something for the pain. He watched his mom brew a tea out of crushed opium poppies, bugleweed, and some other herbs. It was pretty potent stuff. Fortunately Justin knew where to find everything he needed out in the wild.

Now that he was satisfied he found a way to restrain Mannan long enough for the surgery, his next project was a scalpel. That fix was going to have to be simple as well. As Justin figured it, there were lots of things lying around the lab or the office which would be able to cut through the thin flesh of Mannan's hand. There was no need to try smuggling something in when he could easily use a pair of scissors or blade from one of the labs.

Now that everything was settled in Justin's

mind, he had to wait for the ideal time to act. The opportunity presented itself one Friday evening a month later. Most of the staff had gone to workshops in Las Vegas but Justin stayed back to work on the chip. Mannan stayed as well as Justin ensured him he was on the brink of finishing the project. In actuality, he hadn't done anything in the way of advancing GlobalIWitness' goal of implanting a microchip into every man, woman and child. What he had done was to blow an elaborate smokescreen giving Mannan the false impression everything was moving forward at a fast pace. Even though Justin was plotting against the company, everyone still believed he was a company man who would die for the cause. This made Justin's plans all that much easier.

On the morning that he was ready to act he showered, dressed, and packed a small gym bag to take to the office. It wasn't unusual for him to bring a change of clothes or toiletries with him to work since he spent so much time there. Security would think nothing of the bag and there wasn't anything in it that would set off the alarms. Besides a change of clothes he carried a water bottle, half full of his knock out tea, bandages and some strong tape. The last two items were rolled up in a pair of socks. Lastly, he wrapped a bottle of champagne and two glasses in a towel to keep them from breaking. He then placed them in the bag with the other items. He was filled with a nervous excitement; today his life was going to change forever and he couldn't wait.

Before leaving he took a long look around his small house. He stood there waiting for something to kick in, regret, a sense of loss, but nothing happened. Justin turned and walked out slamming the door behind him. The only thing he did feel as he drove off was relief.

Once at work, he headed directly to his office, closed the door, and began to get ready. He rummaged through the mess on his desk and found a pair of scissors but they weren't very sharp. He decided to head to the lab and see if he could find something better. He locked the office door behind him on the off chance someone would come looking for him and snoop in his bag. The lab was only two doors down so he was able to get there and get inside without anyone stopping him. His work was done mostly with virtual imaging and other technology so he didn't keep a lot of other types of supplies at his work area. However, half of the lab was used from time to time by a scientist specializing in genetics. He was working on several other top secret projects for GlobalWitness, of course he never divulged to Justin what exactly those projects were. In fact, he didn't really talk much at all. He always kept to himself and that suited Justin fine. He wasn't concerned with idle chit chat either. Justin didn't even know his name, everyone there just referred to him as Dr. D, so Justin did the same.

The doc's workspace was loaded with just about anything you could think of. It was there that Justin found a sharp pair of surgical scissors and a small unused syringe. He grabbed the two items and headed back to the office. He then packed everything into his duffle bag and shoved it under his desk. Although he needed to begin working, or at least pretend he was working, Justin sat there awhile longer. He mentally walked through the plan several times to make sure he was prepared. He wasn't going to get another chance so this one had to work. Feeling confident, Justin went back to his lab ready to put in a full day's work. As the hours passed, the few staff that had stayed behind began to leave. Soon, it was just Mannan, Justin, and the security officer located at the front desk on the first floor.

Justin spent the last couple of hours of his workday typing up a fake progress report. This, he hoped, would be enough to justify the sparkling wine. He printed the report and tucked it under his arm with the wine bottle. Then he picked up his bag in one hand and grabbed the two glasses with the other. Now, out in the hallway to Mannan's office, he was committed to finish the task. Battling his nerves, he forced himself to continue down the hall. Mannan's office was more of a suite and it was located at the very end of the hall. It seemed like the journey took forever but soon enough he was standing outside Mannan's office. Tapping lightly on the door with the top of the bottle, he pushed it open and walked in.

"Excuse me sir, I hope I'm not interrupting anything," Justin remarked, dropping the bag lightly to the floor beside the door before moving towards the desk.

"No, not at all, what's up?" questioned Mannan barely raising his eyes from the documents on his desk.

"Well, sir I think you'll be interested in this," explained Justin tossing his report on the top of the pile in front of Mannan.

"What's this?" Mannan asked as he picked up the papers and began leafing through them. "Is this what I think it is? He continued excitedly.

"Yes!" Justin echoed his excitement, "I've finished the project and we are ready to move on it sir."

"Excellent, excellent, Walker! I knew we could count on you." He picked up the papers and intently scanned the information they contained. Holding up the bottle of Champagne Justin continued, "That's why I brought this. I thought we could take a little break from work and celebrate." Before Mannan had a chance to respond Justin walked over to the buffet located along the wall behind Mannan's desk, set down the bottle and glasses and started pouring the drinks.

Still reading on the scientific information Justin had given him, he replied slowly, "I don't drink, Walker, it messes with my stomach" Justin almost spilled the Champagne on the floor. What was he going to do now? "I'm sorry sir I didn't realize. But are you sure you won't make an exception just this once. After all, it is a pretty big achievement for GlobalWitness.

"No, Walker I'm sure." He replied as he continued to read.

Justin finished pouring the drinks and took the drug filled syringe from under his shirt where he had taped it earlier. He injected it into Mannan's glass and then dropped the empty syringe on the floor. Using his foot he pushed it under the buffet and out of sight. He stood there stumped for what seemed like an eternity. What was he going to do now? Justin could have kicked himself for not having a contingency plan. He frantically tried to think of something to say but no words came to mind. Fortunately for him, Mannan was preoccupied and barely noticed. Justin was so nervous at this point he could feel the sweat beginning to run down the nape of his neck and into his shirt. He was going to have to knock Mannan out; that was his only option. He glanced at the bottle before dismissing it. That might work but he wasn't sure. "Besides," he thought, "the glass could cause more damage to both of them than just knocking him out." The nearest thing with any weight was a brass award that was on the buffet next to his glass. Taking a deep breath he picked it up and walked up behind his unsuspecting boss. He slowly raised his hand ready to strike.

"You know what Walker," Mannan said, still engrossed in the paperwork. This caught Justin off guard and he almost gasped out loud. "I think I'll have that drink after all."

Justin suppressed a nervous laugh before lowering his arm and returning the trophy to its original spot. His heart was thudding in his chest as the adrenaline kicked in. He had to take several breaths to calm himself before serving the drink. It would be awful if Mannan suspected something now, he was so close! He managed to hand him the glass without spilling. His hands were trembling a little but Mannan didn't seem to notice anything unusual.

"Here's to GlobalIWitness," Justin declared with false bravado, tapping the glass with Mannan's before quickly swallowing its contents. He was relieved when his boss followed suit.

"You know what Walker, I think…" was all Mannan was able to say before slumping forward onto the desk. Wow! Justin was shocked that not only did it work, it worked that fast.

He rushed over to Mannan's lifeless body and checked for a pulse. He was relieved to find it beating strongly. Justin retrieved his duffle bag from where he had dropped it earlier and placed it on the desk. He began pulling the rest of the items from his bag; bandages, alcohol, rope, tape, towels and scissors. His nerves were beginning to kick in so he poured himself another drink. The scissors that he brought were sharp enough but needed to be turned into a scalpel. He accomplished this by opening them as far as they could go and then wrapping tape around one handle and blade. This gave him a way to hold the instrument securely without getting cut himself. He poured alcohol over Mannan's hand and the blade to make sure they were as sterile as possible before taking the makeshift knife and placing it against Mannan's hand. Applying pressure, he made a small cut along the side of the chip. His hand was amazingly steady as he focused on the task. Since the chip wasn't deep, Justin was able to work it out with minimal bleeding. When the operation was complete he cleaned and bandaged the wound before securing Mannan's hands and feet with strong tape. The last thing he wanted was to be interrupted before he had a chance to get away.

He quickly cleaned up the mess he'd made and then gently lowered Mannan onto the floor. His body lay out of sight on the far side of the desk on its side.   That way if security made an unscheduled stop into his office, they wouldn't see. Justin turned off the light and then left the office as if nothing had happened.   He made his way back down the hall but this time stopped in front of the recording room.   Retrieving the handkerchief wrapped microchip from his shirt pocket, he waved it over the security scanner.   There was a gentle "click" and the door opened.

He rushed in and closed it securely behind him before sitting at a computer terminal in the center of the room.   Without wasting any time, Justin began accessing the history files. The moment of truth had finally arrived but, instead of being elated, he faced the moment with trepidation.

The first thing he did was to pull up the files on his parents. Seconds later their faces appeared on the screen with dated video and audio files. He took a deep breath and clicked on the first file, it was of the night the correctors invaded the home. The cams picked up everything. Justin looked into the face of himself, just a boy, being dragged out of his home. They also had the files of his home being torched and his parent's execution. Justin couldn't bear to open the last one; it was just too much.

His hands began to shake from the emotion that the videos stirred. Part of him wanted to stop at that point but he realized this was the only chance he would ever have to view these files. It was now or never. With apprehension he pulled up his grandfather's files. His disappearance had eaten Justin alive for years; always wondering, never knowing. There was a list of files from the day his grandfather had been taken up to days before the farm was invaded. Justin opened the last video in the file. In this video his grandfather was being interrogated. It was obvious that a lot of time had passed. His pap had lost quite a bit of weight. The tape opened in a small room, Justin's grandfather at one side of the table and a corrector almost out of the line of sight on the other.

"Poor Pap," Justin said heartbroken as he looked at the weathered face now bruised and bleeding.

The old man lasted several hours before succumbing to the horrible interrogation tactics. Justin didn't watch the entire video but skipped ahead to the end of the file. Finally, his grandfather broke down and told the correctors what they wanted to hear. "No Pap," Justin whispered in disbelief as he watched his grandfather tell them of their books and their secret hiding place. When they got what they wanted from the old man, a corrector walked up to the table and into eyeshot of the camera. Justin recognized him as the same one who had visited their farm that one day many years ago. He had been on the end of his Pap's gun barrel. "Recognize me Mr. Walker," he said coldly. Before his grandfather was aware of what was happening, the corrector pulled out a hand gun and shot him directly between the eyes. It happened so fast that Justin was unable to look away in time. He gasped at the scene before him horrified.

He sat there several moments in shock. Seeing his family being ripped apart and finding out that his grandfather had been the one responsible was sickening. He couldn't even be mad at him. His poor pap had paid dearly; first the torment of knowing what he had brought upon his family and then death.

He didn't have time to grieve; he needed to move on to the orphanage. What had happened to his friends; his family? He pulled up the orphanage files but had limited information to go by. His fingers shook as he typed in the first name, Carrie, and the date they all arrived at Greenville. Her picture popped up on the screen with an assigned job and apartment in New York. Justin felt the pull on his heart as he saw her beautiful face once more. The picture had been taken on her 18th birthday right before being released from the orphanage. A nurse it said, Carrie had become a nurse. One by one he pulled up the remaining names and wrote down the information he found on a notepad. There were other files associated with each of their names but Justin didn't have time to delve to deeply into any of them. He only got what he needed and moved on.

The last person on his mental list was Daniel. He figured Daniel might be a little harder to find because he had been transferred to another orphanage. Justin was certain though if he could find out which one, he would be able to use his technology expertise to track him down as well. He hurriedly typed in Daniel's name and waited for the results to come up on the screen. It took a little longer than the rest and he was beginning to get nervous because he had been there far too long. Would the effects of the drink wear off before he was done? Justin couldn't honestly answer that question and it ate at him every minute he sat there.

Finally, Daniel's picture popped up on the computer terminal. Terminated was written across his file in large red letters. Justin was so shocked to see the bright red letters that he fell back into his chair unable to catch his breath. He felt as though someone had kicked him in the chest. According to the records, Daniel had been exterminated that day in the orphanage. The report said that he escaped and attacked one of the security guards with a knife. They had no other choice but to shoot him. That didn't sound like Daniel at all. Sure he wanted to get out of there but he would never hurt anyone. Something wasn't right with that report, It couldn't be true. The color drained from Justin's face and he had to close his eyes and take a few deep breaths. He was normally pretty good about controlling his emotions but this was more than just everyday crap. Watching the videos had not just brought Justin pain, it had brought him an understanding of what the government was really up to. The leaders were out of control and there was nothing he could do about it, he was helpless.

He logged out of the database and grabbed his notes and stuffed them into his pants pocket. When he was satisfied his invasion wouldn't be detected, he left the office stopping only long enough to make sure it locked behind him. His entire body was shaking and he wanted to get out of there but he needed to check on Mannan first. He forced himself to slow down and mentally thought about each step he took. His exit from the building needed to be natural as not to alert the guard. Justin slipped back into Mannan's office and walked over to where he had left him laying on the floor. He was still lying on his left side; he hadn't moved at all. Pressing a finger to his right wrist, Justin checked his pulse again. He also took a few minutes to splash some cold water on his face and steady his nerves. He was still feeling queasy but at least some of the color had come back. Satisfied he had everything under control, he took the elevator to the first floor. Mannan would be out for awhile longer so he had nothing to panic about. When he reached his destination and the elevator doors opened, Justin looked like he had every other work day. He walked past the security clutching his gym bag in one hand and his mini personal computer in the other. He barely looked up as he walked by; seemingly intent on the computer screen. It was just a short distance to the door and out to the parking lot.

"Good night Mr. Walker," the guard called out as he opened the front door.

"Good night, see you Monday," responded Justin calmly. Once out of the building he forced himself to walk slowly towards his car until he was out of the sight of the cameras located above the entrance of the building. Once he knew he wasn't going to show up on the security guard's monitors, Justin ran the rest of the way to his car and jumped in the front seat. He shoved his bag over his shoulder into the back. "Home" Justin ordered, once again letting the car handle the drive home. His head was pounding horribly and he felt like he was going to vomit. He knew the government ran a tight ship but this was way more than that. How could he work so closely with them and not realize everything they'd been doing. Or maybe he did know, but he chose to overlook it as long as it didn't touch him directly. He laid his head back on the headrest and closed his eyes, rubbing his eyelids and temples to relieve some of the pain. The trip to his house was pretty quick, only about fifteen minutes. As soon as the car stopped in front of his house, Justin jumped out ready for action. All his thoughts were of getting out of town as quickly as possible. He was so focused he soon forgot about his headache. He couldn't take his car, they would be out looking for him soon and they would be able to use the tracking system in the car to find him. All he could take now was a backpack and rolled up sleeping bag; it was in the trunk filled with food and other things he would need. He quickly pulled on the change of clothes that were folded in the back as well; a black sweatshirt, jeans and tennis shoes. He slipped them on right in the driveway not caring if anyone saw. Nothing really mattered any more anyway. As soon as he finished, Justin started out on foot. Even if he walked all night he wouldn't be able to make it to the cave. His goal was to reach the first supply area he setup in the countryside right past the city limits. Once there, he would have plenty of places to hide.

Justin stayed to the side streets and the shadows as much as possible. He was able to make it outside the city limits and into the dense foliage of the forest in a few hours. He wrapped the sleeping bag around his shoulders and pulled some branches and leaves around him like a small cocoon. Although the night was warm and the brush provided extra insulation, Justin couldn't stop shivering. He was devastated over what he had learned but didn't have time to deal with it now. He just stuffed his emotions away for a better time, if there was one. Sometime during the night Justin managed to fall into a fitful sleep. When he awoke he was completely drained and he only moved to get himself some water, trail mix, and to relieve himself. He needed to lay low for now; the biggest search parties would be sent out at first but would eventually slack off. Or that's what he hoped. He immediately fell back into a deep slumber and when he woke up again it was pitch black; perfect for moving around undetected.

Justin was very familiar with the forest outside the city and had traveled through most of it with his pap and dad during hunting season. Even without the light of the stars, Justin continued onward in confidence. He traveled at night and made camp during the day. It worked out perfectly. It was on that fourth night, just before dawn, that he reached his destination; home. He was exhausted and happy to be able to finally sleep in a bed, even if it was made from straw. Though the shelter wasn't anything fancy, it was dry, warm, and comfortable. He made himself a breakfast of beans and canned meat before washing up and falling into bed. To Justin it was as good as staying at a five star resort. He fell into an exhausted sleep and woke up feeling more like himself the next morning.

Justin spent a few hours walking around the land surrounding his hideout checking for intruders. He wasn't sure if anyone was in the area looking for him but he wanted to make sure. Satisfied that the area was clear and he was alone in his wilderness refuge, Justin headed back to camp. It was kinda weird at first having no job to go to or no one to report to but it only took a few days for Justin to get over it. He had brought along some fishing gear so that evening he was able to catch two small trout for dinner. He cooked it over his campfire with a little butter, salt and pepper. He was also able to pick up some nice greens for a salad. There was nothing like living off of the land. It was the best meal Justin can remember having and he ate every bite. That evening for the first time since his escape, Justin took his Bible from a small crevice in the cave that sufficed very nicely as a shelf and sat down to read by lamplight. He read until his tired eyes couldn't stand any more. That night he slept like a babe; his body, soul and spirit fed and satisfied.

This simple life continued uninterrupted for the next several weeks. Justin spent the days reconnecting with nature and exploring the area.

In the evenings, he read the small Bible trying to find some sort of peace.

Nothing good seems to last forever, or so that's the way Justin felt when he was awakened early one morning by the sounds of dogs and men crashing through the underbrush. He didn't have to guess, he knew they were correctors and they were close. He jumped out of bed, threw his clothes and shoes on and then ran outside. He could hear them off in the distance but they were definitely coming his way. Overhead he could hear the sounds of a chopper but was unable to see it through the dense canopy of trees. "Well, if I can't see them, then they can't see me either," Justin reasoned. He needed to get out of there fast!

He left everything behind him and began running as fast as he could in the opposite direction. He had a head start but it wasn't really going to make a difference if the dogs got a whiff of his scent. They would catch up and overtake him in minutes. His brain was working as fast as his feet as he tried to think of a strategy to get away. The only thing he could think of was finding a body of water, it didn't matter how small. If he could cross it perhaps it would be enough for the dogs to lose him.

With that thought in mind and his own little creek far behind him, Justin turned abruptly to the right and ran straight towards the stream he and his father used to fish every summer. His was running out of steam but he continued to push on. He just needed to make it over a small grassy hill and he would be there. As he reached the top and saw the sparkling water before him he sighed with relief. He rushed into the cold water without slowing down and began running downstream. The water was only ankle high but the rocks beneath his shoes were covered in algae and slime making the journey slow. A couple of times he needed to stop and steady himself because his feet slid causing him to lose his balance. He could hear the dogs barking even louder now; he knew they were getting close. Justin exited the stream on the opposite side of the bank, running a little slower now. He was exhausted but he couldn't stop for but for a minute here and there. There wasn't any time for a long rest, not if he had any hopes of escaping.

He slowly zigzagged up the side of the next hill, stopping periodically to catch his breath. He grabbed on to the brush and pulled himself onward and upwards. When he got to the top he leaned up against a tree and closed his eyes, just for a second. This part of the forest was pretty well overgrown, the trails hadn't been used in years and they were completely covered. Because of this, the going was even more treacherous. Now he was moving a little more slowly, carefully stepping over the growth on the forest's floor.

It didn't seem to matter how much progress he made, the sounds of the dogs and correctors continued to get louder. Tripping over the roots of a tree, Justin tumbled down an embankment. When he reached the bottom and stopped rolling, he lay on his back looking up at the sky. Overhead the chopper hovered; he didn't have a chance. But, Justin refused to give up. He got to his feet and limping, continued to run. He wasn't going to stop and make it easy for them. If they wanted him bad enough they were going to have to work for it.

Another mile in the chase Justin found himself on the rocky edge of an embankment; Summit Point. Justin and his friends used to sit at the top and throw rocks over the edge, trying to guess how high it was by counting how long it took for them to reach the bottom. After tossing a few they realized it was so high they would never hear the sound of the impact. This was the worst place he could have ended up; there wasn't any place to go but down. "I guess it's over," he thought as he looked down into the precipice. All he could see were the tops of the overgrown trees spread out like a welcoming blanket; waiting to catch him. Justin stood at the edge, the sounds of the correctors now screaming at him from behind. He was actually pretty calm considering what he was about to do. He felt the summer breeze brush across his face and the heat from the noon day sun warming his skin. Everything felt and smelled clean and alive; it was so peaceful here. Justin just wished it could have lasted a little longer. He closed his eyes breathing in the fresh air deeply; inhale, exhale, inhale, exhale, inhale; he took one last deep breath before falling face forward into the earth below.

10
BEGINNING OF THE END

Justin felt an unusual heaviness in his chest, almost like someone or something was sitting on it. His breathing was unnatural too, he could feel an object lying across his tongue running towards the back of his throat forcing air in and then back out again. He moved his head to the side and pushed with his tongue but the object refused to budge. Opening his mouth a little wider he tried to speak but could only muster up a low moan. "Where am I?" he thought. He couldn't seem to make any sense of it. His head hurt really badly and every thought took effort to form. It was like he was pushing though a thick fog trying to find his way back to reality. What made it worse was his inability to see his surroundings. As hard as he tried, it seemed impossible to pull his swollen eyelids apart. It was only after numerous attempts that he manage to peer through small slits. What he saw took him completely aback; he was looking directly into the beautiful grey eyes of an angel. She peered intently at his face and gently brushed back his hair. His eyesight was working as poorly as the rest of him, it moved in and out of focus making him feel even more disoriented. Seeing the distress in his face, the angel put a finger up to her lips to quiet him and bent down next to him, her hair brushing up against the side of his face, "It's ok Justin, just rest," she whispered. She was so close that Justin could smell the fragrance of her perfume. It reminded him of the honeysuckle and lilacs that grew in his back yard at the farm. Every time Justin walked out the door of the house he would get a whiff of the sweet flowers. And sometimes his mother would bring some of the blossoms into the house. The aroma would be carried throughout their home by the summer breeze. It was a soothing memory and caused Justin to visibly relax. The angel continued to look at him gently, her face seemed so familiar. But, Justin couldn't quite think of who she reminded him of. And then, like a bolt of lightning, he had it! "Carrie," Justin thought, unable to voice his revelation. The angel injected something into his IV and soon Justin slipped back into unconsciousness.

Justin was walking in a field of tall grass with his grandfather. It was in the middle of the day and the sun was bright and warm. The scent of flowers mingled with sweet vernal grass filled his nostrils. Each step he took unleashed more of its marvelous scent. He took a deep breath and smiled broadly. Right then he stopped dead in his tracks and looked at his grandfather curiously.

"Am I dead?" He asked while looking down at his own body, noticing it was a lot smaller than he was used to. Besides shrinking in stature he was wearing his stripped t-shirt with the ice-cream stain on the front. He was back to being ten years old again. He pinched himself and winced slightly.

Noticing his behavior his grandfather chuckled, "No Justin, you're just asleep right now."

Justin looked up at him soberly remembering the cares of the world he had come from, "You're not really my grandfather are you?"

"No", the man answered as he turned and smiled tenderly at him. The glare of the sun behind his shoulders cast an ethereal glow about him.

Justin squinted and put his hand up to his eyes to shade them from the brightness, "Who are you then?"

"You know the answer to that question already, don't you son?" the man answered patiently.

"Yes, I guess I do," He replied thoughtfully.

"I have to go now Justin. Besides, it's about time you wake up." The man began to turn and walk away causing Justin to panic. "Can't I just stay here? I don't want to go back," He argued.

"You can't stay, there's a lot more I need for you to do," He answered.

"I don't think I can do it, not by myself anyway." Justin's voice broke with emotion, his big brown eyes filling with unshed tears.

"I know it isn't easy Justin but you need to understand something, you've never been alone; I've been standing right beside you the entire time waiting." He explained compassionately.

Justin rubbed his eyes with the back of his had to get rid of any evidence he had been crying. He looked up at the man in wonder and asked, "Waiting for what?"

"For you to ask," the man replied simply.

The dream ended as Justin woke up for the second time. He wasn't greeted by his earlier vision but by the head nurse, who was far from angelic. "Dorothy" was displayed on the pin attached to the collar of her uniform. It was discolored from years of use and spotted with a red substance that looked like the spaghetti sauce from one of her lunches; or at least Justin hoped that's what it was. She had broad shoulders and arms bigger than his. "I don't think I'd want to mess with her," Justin thought as he watched her pick up the guy in the next bed and roll him over like a rag doll while changing his sheets. Around her neck hung a monitoring device capable of doing complete diagnostics on a patient with one pass over. And a small camera was clipped on the side of her uniform hat. The camera was standard issue which sent audio and video to the Global Life History Bank. Everything these days was recorded and the old laws of confidentiality and privacy were thrown out the window when the new order was established. For our own good of course!

When Dorothy finished with the other patient

she turned to face Justin. She seemed a little startled to see him looking back at her. "Bout time you got round to waking up Mr. Walker," she said roughly as she began doing a scan on his broken and bruised body. "You're one lucky man you are," she continued.

"Luck had nothing to do with it," he croaked, his throat dry and sore.

"Call it what you like," she answered, "but you should be a dead man."

"What happened," Justin squeaked out. The memory of the incident still evaded him.

"Not now Mr. Walker," she said brushing him off, "You'll have plenty of time later, plenty of time."

She lifted Justin's head and offered him some water before injecting a sedative into his IV solution. Justin was out again in a matter of a few minutes. This time his sleep was deep and dreamless; it was a healing sleep that he needed desperately.

Justin slipped in and out of consciousness aided by the medication for the next couple of weeks. This was necessary in order to heal his body without a great deal of pain. Eventually he began to get stronger and was able to stay awake most of the day. It was at that time Dorothy decided to fill him in.

Justin remembered the leap off the ledge but

nothing afterwards. That was probably for the best though. Dorothy explained that, once he had made it through the first layer of overhanging branches, Justin had come face to face with a stone ledge. Lucky for him, the ledge was not only big enough to stop his descent; it was covered with dense brush which gave him a little cushioning. Of course the fall was bad enough to crush the bones in his right leg, break a few ribs, cause some internal bleeding, and put him in a coma for almost a month. But that was nothing compared to what it could have been. He could have died on impact. His survival was nothing less than a miracle; Justin was convinced of that.

Now that he was thinking a little more clearly, Justin wondered about the vision he had. Had it been real? Was it Carrie? But then, that would be impossible. In his heart he hoped he would see Carrie again but it didn't appear to be likely to happen. He just wasn't thinking straight, the drugs they were giving him for pain made his mind go in all kind of crazy directions. He had to really control himself because he was afraid that he might let something slip. He might incriminate himself before he ever got to court.

Every evening after he finished the awful hospital dinner, and the nurse took the last medical readings, Justin would slip out of bed and drag himself over to the window. There was a chair next to his bed with rollers on the bottom. It took some time but he eventually managed to slide off of the bed and into the waiting chair. After that it was easy enough. He could just scoot the chair over to the window. Justin stayed there for a couple of hours before heading back to his bed. He knew the nurse would be in soon and he didn't need any more trouble than he already had. Besides, the pain in his leg was usually bad by then. He was only too happy to be lying down again.

There was no one there to report his deeds to the night nurse because his roommate had been removed weeks earlier. Justin figured they didn't want him to be talking with other patients in the hospital; he might contaminate someone with his anti-government ideas.

Besides the removal of his roommate, Dorothy had become closed mouthed. The most Justin ever got out of her lately was "lay still while I check your readings". Not what you would call stimulating conversation. He was getting pretty bored and longed to be outdoors again. That's why, despite the horrible pain in his leg, he made his way to the window. The hospital room was only a couple stories off the ground and offered a good view of the hustle and bustle of the town. Every once in awhile, someone in the crowd would glace upwards towards the window and stop as if they could see him there. Justin instinctively jerked backwards into his chair every time. It wasn't like they were going to do anything, but it made him feel extremely vulnerable.

The weeks progressed about the same, each day he felt stronger and more like a caged animal. The regular readings taken by the nurses showed Justin was healing rather nicely. Several weeks later he had nothing to show for his accident except a bad limp and some bruises. Unfortunately, now he was healed, he would be brought to court and be judged.

Although Justin hadn't seen them, he knew the correctors were right outside his hospital room the entire time waiting. The food service attendee would always stop outside his room after delivering his meal and hand two others to someone just out of sight. Justin was hurt but he wasn't stupid. He knew he wasn't going to be forgotten.

When that day did come two weeks later, the controllers entered his room and guarded the room from the inside until he was dressed and they received his discharge papers. They weren't going to let him out of their sight now; he was their responsibility once the papers touched their hands.

They took an elevator down to the ground floor and exited the front of the building. Their car was there waiting for them. They opened the back passenger door and motioned for Justin to take a seat. Then, his two "bodyguards" were kind enough to give him a ride to the courthouse. They sat stone-faced and silent in the front of the vehicle until Justin began to speak to them.

"Don't you think this whole thing is a little ridiculous? Why did anyone bother taking me to the hospital in the first place? You could have just left me there on the ledge to die," Justin asked pointedly. He didn't understand why they bothered with the time and expense of rescuing and hospitalizing him. Knowing how corrupt the government and law enforcement was, he was surprised they didn't just shoot him and be done with it.

"Everyone deserves their day in court Mr. Walker, even criminals such as yourself," the driver explained, "We wouldn't want to deprive you or your accusers of that opportunity."

"Yeah, I can tell you're looking out for our best interests," Justin scoffed, "Just like the government did for my parents, my grandfather and all those poor kids at the orphanage."

"You know how many times we hear this crap," the other corrector chimed in, "People break the law and then they whine to us when they get caught. We're really not interested in anything you have to say. We've heard it all before."

"Don't try to pretend this system is fair, that everyone you bring to "justice" is guilty. The government is slaughtering innocent people every day and you help them do it." Justin continued, his voice rising in anger.

The driver pushed a button on the consol of the vehicle and a partition slid up dividing the front half of the car from the back. Before it closed and blocked off the sound, the driver added, "One thing I've learned over the years Mr. Walker, never argue with a crazy man." Justin hit the back of the seat in anger and frustration. Nothing he could say or do would change the minds of these puppets. They were so brainwashed by the system it was going to take a miracle. But, he'd already experienced one of those so it might not be so farfetched.

The rest of the journey was uneventful since Justin couldn't even talk to the correctors. He sat there trying to prepare himself for what he was going to face. As if going to your impending death wasn't bad enough, the medication he got at the hospital started to wear off and his leg was throbbing. He kept trying to reposition it but nothing worked. "Unbelievable," he sighed under his breath. Fortunately they reached their destination minutes later. The car slowed and then came to a complete stop in Courthouse Plaza directly in front of the courthouse. The correctors quickly exited the car but Justin had to wait for one of them to open his door. The interior in the back of the vehicle was smooth and devoid of any window or door controls. They weren't going to take any chances that he'd get out and run away, not that he'd be doing any running any time soon. Seconds later the door popped open and a corrector looked at him with a smirk and said, "We're here Mr. Walker, can't wait to get started!"

11
THE REBIRTH

"Mr. Walker...Mr. Walker!" the Speaker shouted startling him, "The proceedings are about over...do you have anything to say in your defense?"

Justin shook his head trying to clear his thoughts. He had spent most of the trial lost in memories. His head began to spin as he tried to think of a response to the speaker. These would most likely be his last words so he wanted them to be worth saying. He bowed his head, eyes closed, and took a deep breath. He was trying to collect himself but not in the way most thought. "You said you were here with me," Justin whispered, barely more than a breath, "I need you now, please help me!"

All of a sudden, he was overcome with a calm that he'd never experienced before. He slowly stood up to address the committee and the others in the courtroom.

"In my defense?" He said softly, leaning on the back of the chair for support, "What can I say...I'm guilty of all these things." He turned his eyes to face each of his accusers directly, "What you say about me is absolutely true."

"What! This is craziness!" shouted the speaker, "No one has ever come to be judged and actually admitted guilt! Do you understand what you are saying?"

Justin had only just begun, "Yes..yes I understand. If you will permit, I would like to continue."

The speaker was obviously flustered, her face was flushed and she looked very uncomfortable, "Get on with it, we don't have all day!"

Justin began slowly, softly, but his words increased with passion as he spoke. "I *am* guilty of all these things and even more...I can only ask for forgiveness for what I've done," he looked directly at each of their surprised faces as he spoke.

"Is this your defense? Do you really think asking for forgiveness is going to get you off the hook for everything you've done?" the supreme judge interjected. He usually didn't interfere with the proceedings unless there was a problem; and this was a problem. "If you don't have any testimony to prove your innocence your words are meaningless."

"You don't understand," Justin continued boldly, "I'm not asking any of you for forgiveness. The only forgiveness I need comes from my Father."

"Your father? What does he have to do with this? Your father is dead!" one of the committee members shouted losing his composure. That was enough to send the rest of the room into a spin. They all began arguing and talking at once; it was total chaos. Some thought that the accident and the stress of being judged were too much; he had lost his mind. Others thought it he was going to try to use some kind of insanity defense. The general consensus however was that they wanted this hearing to be over with.

Justin wasn't deterred; he continued speaking loudly, his voice rising above the chaos. "I'm speaking of my heavenly Father," he continued, "Only by the blood of his son, Jesus Christ...who I now call Lord are these things able to be forgiven." With that statement the room immediately became silent. Everyone looked at him like he was totally insane. Even the supreme judge seemed to be at a loss for words.

Not even noticing the change in the room, Justin continued passionately, "Lord, I'm asking for your help now! I need you now, please!" he continued, tears streaming down his face. Looking upwards toward the ceiling Justin held his hands outstretched, "I know what you meant Jesus, you *were* there with me. Please forgive me for waiting so long to come to you....I'm coming now!"

He turned to look directly into the speaker's eyes and spoke with confidence. "I call upon Him now..dear God forgive me...forgive me for forgetting about You, forgive me for being part of this corrupt world, forgive me all my sins."

The room was silent...for several very long

moments. Justin slowly put down his hands and waited for a response, any response. It didn't matter anymore. He knew that even if he was executed today he would be with his dear Savior; that's all that mattered.

The supreme judge cleared his throat and began shuffling through the stack of papers in front of him. His face began to turn slightly red, either from anger or embarrassment, Justin wasn't sure which. Justin just waited calmly while he pulled himself together. Finally, he placed his folded hands over the stack of papers and asked in confusion, "Who are you and what are you doing in my courtroom?"

"What?! What are you talking about?" Justin stuttered. That wasn't what he expected in the least. "I'm Justin Walker, remember you called me here to be judged. "

"I don't remember any Justin Walker" He turned to look directly at the controllers, "Is this some sort of a joke?" His voice began to rise in anger. "Does anyone here know this man? Everyone in the room was just as confused; they shook their heads in denial and shifted nervously in their seats. They were more concerned as to why they were sitting there rather than with who Justin was. Their minds raced, "If he wasn't about to be judged, did the court have something in surprise for one of them?"

Justin slowly walked over to the row of accusers

now occupying the chairs against the wall and stood in front of them, trying to figure out what was going on. Even his boss looked at him blankly; the incident at the office apparently completely forgotten. He turned back to the committee and said, "Your correctors brought me here. How else would I be able to get in? I'm Justin Walker..W..A..L..K..E..R....Walker."

"Mr. Phillips, pull up this young man's record before I lose my patience," the supreme judge ordered.

"Already on it sir...hmmmm...let's see...Justin Walker. It's right here. This is strange...very strange..." he replied slowly.

"What are you talking about? What does that damn computer have to say?!" The supreme judge shouted pounding his fist on the table.

"Why...his record is as clean as a newborn...there's nothing there." Mr. Phillips continued in puzzlement.

"What?! That can't be right," he said getting up to come over and look at the screen. Several puzzling seconds later he said, "Well Mr. Walker there seems to be some sort of mistake here. We have nothing against you. I really don't know what to do other than to apologize, this has never happened before."

Wanting to put the blame on someone he turned his attention back to the correctors, "I'm sorry for any inconvenience that the correctors may have caused. I assure you they will be dealt with strictly." Both of the correctors baulked at the statement. They knew what "being dealt with" meant.

Justin was feeling so good at that point he even felt bad for them, "There is no need...I'm sure it was an honest mistake. If you don't mind though, I'd really like to go home."

"Of course, of course, you are free to leave." The supreme judge stated with authority, "But before you go I want to commend you on your record; you are an exemplary citizen and an example to us all. Keep up the good work!" And then he turned to the much relieved controllers and added "Make sure this young man makes it outside all right.

Justin was quickly led out of the building by two very thankful correctors and once more stood at the top of the courthouse steps. "Thank you God!" he shouted, not caring if he was observed. After all he had a clean slate and His father was the God of the Universe; he had nothing to worry about anymore.

He slowly walked down the steps, his leg still very sore. Once at the bottom he stopped to contemplate his next more. He needed a plan but first, he needed some sleep. "I guess I'll head home and worry about it later," Justin thought. He knew that he had to heal a bit more before he started off on another adventure. After he was back on his feet, he was going to start finding his friends; Carrie would be the first. If God was capable of saving him, Justin was sure the rest of his adopted family wasn't beyond His reach. It would be a new beginning for all of them too. The huge grin that spread across his face reflected the joy and excitement that he felt.

Justin raised his hand to flag down a passing public transport vehicle. A black car pulled up in front of him instead. As soon as it rolled to a stop, a gentleman wearing an expensive suit stepped out blocking Justin's way. "Excuse me," Justin remarked brushing past him. "What's your hurry Mr. Walker?" He said to Justin's retreating form.

Justin stopped in his tracks and spun around to face the man, his back to the car door. "I'm sorry, you don't look familiar. Do I know you?"

"No, "he responded, "But you will before long."

Justin didn't even have time to respond to that strange statement. Just then a black cloth sack was shoved over his head from behind and he was pulled backwards into the car. The abrupt movement caused Justin to cry out as the pain coursed up his leg. He tried to fight back as several sets of hands held him down, but was unable to escape their grasp. Then, he felt a sharp pinch in the back of his left hand. Seconds later a warm

sensation flooded his body and then there was
nothing but darkness.

The end.

ABOUT THE AUTHOR

Elaine Reeves lives in San Diego with her husband and their two furry children; Cisco and Buttercup. She grew up in western Pennsylvania but moved to California after meeting the love of her life. They have been happily married now for eight years.

Elaine plans to continue writing God inspired books as long as He provides her with the content. Her last book Thanksgiving: A Tale of Salvation is currently available through Amazon.com.

20785426R00091

Made in the USA
Charleston, SC
24 July 2013